"Not yet."

The soft demand froze her in place. In that moment she registered that Constantine wasn't just angry, he was furious.

She had seen him furious only once before—the day they had broken up—but on that occasion he had been icily cool and detached. The fact that his formidable control had finally slipped and he was clearly in danger of losing his temper ratcheted the tension up several notches.

A heady sense of anticipation gripped her. She had the feeling that for the first time she was going to see the real Constantine and not the controlled tycoon who had a calculator in place of a heart.

His gaze dropped to her mouth and she was suddenly unbearably aware that he intended to kiss her.

Dear Reader,

The idea for The Pearl House miniseries had its beginnings with strong-willed Sienna Ambrosi, on a mission to keep the family's luxury Sydney-based pearl business afloat. Pretty and resourceful, with a focused, perfectionist streak, she is just the kind of character I like; she never gives up. Already walking a financial tightrope, Sienna gets hit by a serious reversal by the name of Constantine Atraeus.

The Atraeus and Ambrosi families have a history, and so did Sienna and Constantine, until debt terminated their previous engagement.

It's kind of ironic, then, that debt should bring them back together, although *useful* would be the term that Constantine would use. Underneath his ruthless exterior, he's a nice guy with a sense of humor, and he has never forgotten Sienna. He had been trying to figure out an excuse to see her again when out of the blue her company literally dropped into his hands.

Now, if only she'd just see him, instead of his bottom line....

Fiona

FIONA BRAND

A BREATHLESS BRIDE

Recycling programs
for this product may
not exist in your area.

ISBN-13: 978-0-373-73167-1

A BREATHLESS BRIDE

Copyright © 2012 by Fiona Gillibrand

www.Harlequin.com

Printed in U.S.A.

Books by Fiona Brand

Harlequin Desire

A Breathless Bride #2154

Silhouette Intimate Moments

Cullen's Bride #914
Heart of Midnight #977
Blade's Lady #1023
Marrying McCabe #1099
Gabriel West: Still the One #1219
High-Stakes Bride #1403

Silhouette Books

Sheiks of Summer
  "Kismet"

*The Pearl House

Other titles by this author available in ebook format.

FIONA BRAND

lives in the sunny Bay of Islands, New Zealand. Now that both of her sons are grown, she continues to love writing books and gardening. After a life-changing time in which she met Christ, she has undertaken study for a bachelor of theology and has become a member of The Order of St. Luke, Christ's healing ministry.

For the Lord. Thank you.

On finding one pearl of great value,
he went and sold all that he had and bought it.
—*Matthew* 13:46

One

With a wolf-cold gaze, Constantine Atraeus scanned the mourners attending Roberto Ambrosi's funeral, restlessly seeking...and finding.

With her long blond hair and dark eyes, elegantly curved body and rich-list style, Roberto's daughter Sienna stood out like an exotic bird among ravens.

His jaw compressing at the unmistakable evidence of her tears, Constantine shook off an unwilling surge of compassion. And memories. No matter how innocent Sienna looked, he couldn't allow himself to forget that his ex-fiancée was the new CEO of her family's failing pearl empire. She was first and foremost an Ambrosi. Descended from a once wealthy family, the Ambrosis were noted for two things: their luminous good looks and their focus on the bottom line.

In this case, his bottom line.

"Tell me you're not going after her now."

Constantine's brother Lucas, still jet-lagged from a long-haul flight from Rome to Sydney, levered himself out of the Audi Constantine had used to pick up both of his brothers from the airport.

In the Sydney office for two days of meetings, Lucas was dressed for business, although he'd long since abandoned the jacket and tie. Zane, who was already out of the car and examining the funeral crowd, was dressed in black jeans and a black shirt, a pair of dark glasses making him look even more remote.

Lucas was edgily good-looking, so much so that the media dogged him unmercifully. Zane, who was technically their half brother, and who had spent time on the streets of L.A. as a teenager before their father had found him, simply looked dangerous. The outer packaging aside, Constantine was confident that when it came to protecting his family's assets both of his brothers were sharks.

Constantine shrugged into the jacket he'd draped over the back of the driver's seat as he watched Sienna accept condolences, his frustration edged by a surge of emotion that had nothing to do with temper.

Grimly, he considered that the physical attraction that had drawn him away from The Atraeus Group's head office on Medinos, when his legal counsel could have handled the formalities, was clouding his judgment.

No, that wasn't it. Two years ago Constantine had finally learned to separate sexual desire from business. He was no longer desperate.

This time if and when Sienna Ambrosi came to his bed, it would be on his terms, not hers.

"I'm not here to put flowers on Roberto's grave."

"Or allow her to grieve. Ever heard of tomorrow?" Lucas shrugged into his jacket and slammed the door of the Audi.

Constantine winced at Lucas's treatment of the expensive car. Lucas hadn't been old enough to remember the bad old days when the Atraeus family had been so poor they hadn't been able to afford a car, but Constantine could. His father's discovery of a rich gold mine on the Mediterranean island of Medinos hadn't altered any of his childhood memories. He would never forget what it had felt like to have nothing. "When it comes to the Ambrosi family, tomorrow will be too late." Resignation laced his tone as he eyed the press gathering like vultures at a feast. "Besides, it looks like the story has already been leaked. Bad timing or not, I want answers."

And to take back the money Roberto Ambrosi had conned out of their dying father while Constantine had been out of the country.

Funeral or not, he would unravel the scam he had discovered just over a week ago. After days of unreturned calls and hours of staking out the apparently empty residences of the Ambrosi family, his patience was gone, as was the desire to finish this business discreetly.

Lucas fell into step beside Constantine as he started toward the dispersing mourners. Grimly, Constantine noted that Lucas's attention was fixed on the younger Ambrosi daughter, Carla.

"Are you certain Sienna's involved?"

Constantine didn't bother to hide his incredulity.

Just what were the odds that the woman who had agreed to marry him two years ago, knowing that her father was leveraging an under-the-table deal with his, hadn't known about Roberto's latest scam? "She knows."

"You know what Roberto was like—"

"More than willing to exploit a dying man."

Constantine made brief eye contact with the two bodyguards who had accompanied them in a separate vehicle. The protection wasn't his choice, but as the CEO of a multibillion-dollar corporation, he'd had to deal with more than his share of threats.

As they neared the graveside, Constantine noted the absence of male family members or escorts. The wealthy and powerful Ambrosi family, who had employed his grandfather as a gardener, now only consisted of Margaret—Roberto's widow—the two daughters, Sienna and Carla, and a collection of elderly aunts and distant cousins.

As he halted at the edge of the mounded grave, the heavy cloud, which had been steadily building overhead, slid across the face of the midday sun and Sienna's dark gaze finally locked with his. In that fractured moment, something close to joy flared, as if she had forgotten that two years ago, when it had come down to a choice between him or the money, she had gone for the cash.

For a long, drawn out moment, Constantine was held immobile by a shifting sense of déjà vu, a powerful moment of connection he had been certain he would never again feel.

Something kicked in his chest, an errant pulse of emotion, and instead of dragging his gaze away he allowed himself to be caught, entangled...

A split second later a humid gust of wind sent leaves flying. In the few moments it took Sienna to anchor the honeyed fall of her hair behind one ear, the dreamy incandescence that had ensnared him—fooled him—so completely two years ago was gone, replaced by stunned disbelief.

A kick of annoyance that, evidently, despite all of his unreturned calls, Sienna had failed to register his presence in Sydney, was edged by relief. For a moment there, he had almost lost it, but now they were both back on the same, familiar page.

Constantine terminated the eye contact and transferred his attention to the freshly mounded soil, now covered by lavish floral tributes. Reasserting his purpose, reminding himself.

Roberto Ambrosi had been a liar, a thief and a con man, but Constantine would give him his due: he had known when to make his exit.

Sienna, however, had no such avenue of escape.

Sienna's heart slammed hard as Constantine closed the distance between them. Just for a few moments, exhausted by sadness and worn-out from fighting the overwhelming relief that she no longer had to cope with her father's gambling addiction, she had let the grimness of the cemetery fade.

She'd trained herself to be a relentlessly positive thinker, but even for her, the wispy daydream had been unusually creative: a reinvention of the past, where love came first, instead of somewhere down a complex list of assets and agendas. Then she had turned and for a disorienting moment, the future she had once thought was hers—and which she had needed with a fierceness that still haunted her—had taken on dazzling life. Constantine.

The reality of his clean, powerful features—coal-black hair brushing broad shoulders and the faintly resinous male scent that never failed to make her heart pound—had shocked her back to reality.

"What are you doing here?" she demanded curtly. Since the embarrassing debacle two years ago, the Ambrosis and the Atraeuses had preserved an icy distance. Constantine was the last person she expected to see at her father's funeral, and the least welcome.

Constantine's fingers closed around hers. The warm, slightly rough, skin-on-skin contact sent a hot, tingling shock through her. She inhaled sharply and a hint of the cologne that had sent her spiraling into the past just seconds ago made her stomach clench.

Constantine was undeniably formidable and gorgeous. Once he had fascinated her to the point that she had broken her cardinal rule. She had stopped thinking in favor of feeling. Big mistake.

Constantine had been out of her league, period. He was too rich, too powerful and, as she had found out to her detriment, utterly focused on protecting his family's business empire.

Bitterly, she reflected that the tabloids had it right. Ruthless in business, ditto in bed. The CEO of The Atraeus Group was a catch. Just don't "bank" on a wedding.

He leaned forward, close enough that his cleanly shaven jaw almost brushed her cheek. For an electrifying moment she thought he was actually going to kiss her, then the remoteness of his expression wiped that thought from her mind.

"We need to talk." His voice was deep and curt—a cosmopolitan mix of accents that revealed that, his Mediterranean heritage aside, he had been educated in the States. "Five minutes. In the parking lot." Jerking her fingers free, Sienna stepped back, her high heels sinking into the soft ground.

Meet with the man who had proposed one week, then discarded her the next because he believed she was a calculating gold digger?

That would be when hell froze over.

"We don't have anything to discuss."

"Five minutes. Be there."

Stomach tight, she stared at the long line of his back as he strolled away through the ranks of marble headstones. Peripherally she noticed Lucas and Zane, Constantine's two brothers, flanking him. Two security guards kept onlookers and the reporters who inevitably hounded the Atraeus family at bay.

Tension hummed through her at the presence of both brothers and the security. The bodyguards were a reality check, underlining the huge gulf between her life and his.

She registered a brief touch on her arm. Her sister, Carla. With an effort of will, Sienna shook off the shock of Constantine's presence and her own unsettling reactions. Her father's sudden death and the messy financial fallout that followed had consumed every waking moment for the past few days. Despite that, all it had taken had been one fractured moment looking into Constantine's gaze and she had forgotten where she was and why.

Carla frowned. "You look as white as a sheet. Are you all right?"

"I'm fine." Desperate to regain her equilibrium, Sienna dug in her purse, found her compact and checked her makeup. After the tears in church and the humid heat, any trace of the light makeup she had applied that morning was gone. Her hair was tousled and her eyes were red-rimmed—the exact opposite of her usual cool, sophisticated façade.

Carla—who was far more typically Medinian than Sienna in appearance with glossy dark hair and stunning light blue eyes that stopped people in their tracks—watched the Atraeus brothers, an odd expression in her eyes. "What are they doing here? Please don't tell me you're seeing Constantine again."

Sienna snapped the compact closed and dropped it into her purse. "Don't worry, I'm not crazy."

Just confused.

"Then what did they want?"

Carla's clipped demand echoed Sienna's question, although she couldn't afford the luxury of either anger or passion. For the sake of her family and their company, she had to be controlled and unruffled, no matter how worried she felt. "Nothing."

Constantine's series of commands replayed itself in her mind. Another gust, this one laced with fat droplets of rain, snapped her numbed brain back into high gear. Suddenly she formed a connection that made her pulse pound and her stomach hollow out.

Oh, damn. She needed to think, and quickly.

Over the past three days, she had spent long hours sifting through her father's private papers and financial records. She had found several mystifyingly large deposits she couldn't match to any of the business figures. Money had come in over a two-month period. A very large amount. The money had been used to prop up Ambrosi Pearls' flagging finances and cover her father's ongoing gambling debts, but she had no idea of its source. At first she thought the money had to be winnings, but the similar amounts had confused her. Roberto Ambrosi had won large sums of money in the past, but the amounts had differed wildly.

Now Constantine wanted a conversation.

Desperate to deny the conclusion that was forming, and to distract Carla, who was still locked on the Atraeus brothers like a heat-seeking missile, she craned around, searching for their mother. "Mom needs help."

Carla had also spotted the reporter chatting to Margaret Ambrosi, who was exhausted and still a little shaky from the sedatives the doctor had prescribed so she could sleep. "Oh, heck. I'll get her. It's time we left anyway. We were supposed to be at Aunt Via's for lunch ten minutes ago."

A private family lunch at the apartment of their father's

sister, Octavia, not a wake, which Sienna had decreed was an unnecessary luxury.

The last four days since her father had collapsed and died from a heart attack had been a roller-coaster ride, but that didn't change the reality. The glory days of Ambrosi Pearls, when her grandfather had transferred the company from the disaster zone Medinos had become during World War II to Sydney, were long gone. She had to balance the need to bolster business confidence by giving the impression of wealth and stability against the fact that they were operating on a shoestring budget. Luckily, her father had had a small insurance policy, enough to cover basic funeral expenses, and she'd had the excuse of Margaret Ambrosi's poor health to veto any socializing.

Her gaze narrowed. "Tell Via I'm not going to be able to make it for lunch. I'll see you at home later on."

After she had gotten rid of Constantine.

Constantine sent a brooding glance at the sky as he unlocked the Audi and settled in to wait for Sienna.

From the backseat Zane crossed his arms over his chest and coolly surveyed the media who were currently trying to bluff their way past Constantine's security. "I can see she still really likes you."

Constantine stifled his irritation. At twenty-four, Zane was several years his junior. Sometimes the chasm seemed much wider than six years. "This is business." Not pleasure.

Lucas slid into the passenger-side seat. "Did you get a chance to discuss the loan with Roberto?"

The words *before he died* hung in the air.

Constantine dragged at his tie. "Why do you think he had the heart attack?"

Apparently Roberto had suffered from a heart condition. Instead of showing up at Constantine's house, as arranged for the meeting that he himself had requested, he had been seated at a blackjack table. When he hadn't shown up, Constantine had made some calls and found out that Roberto had gone directly to the casino, apparently feverishly trying to win the money he needed.

Constantine had sent his personal assistant Tomas to collect Ambrosi, because going himself would have attracted unwanted media attention. Tomas had arrived to find that seconds after a substantial win the older man had become unwell. Tomas had called an ambulance. Minutes later Roberto had clutched at his chest and dropped like a stone.

Constantine almost had a heart attack himself when he had heard. Contrary to reports that he was ruthless and unfeeling, he had been happy to discuss options with Roberto, but it was not just about him. He had his family and the business to consider and Roberto Ambrosi had conned his father.

Lucas's expression was thoughtful. "Does Sienna know that you arranged to meet with her father?"

"Not yet."

"But she will."

"Yep." Constantine stripped off his tie, which suddenly felt like a noose, and yanked at the top two buttons of his shirt.

He wanted to engage Sienna's attention, which was the whole point of him dealing with the problem directly.

It was a safe bet that, after practically killing her old man, he had it by now.

Thunder rumbled overhead. Sienna walked quickly toward her car, intending to grab the umbrella she had stashed on the backseat.

As she crossed the parking lot a van door slid open. A reporter stepped onto the steaming asphalt just ahead of her and lifted his camera. Automatically, her arm shot up, fending off the flash.

A second reporter joined the first. Spinning on her heel, Sienna changed direction, giving up on the notion of staying dry. Simultaneously, she became aware that another news van had just cruised into the parking lot.

This wasn't part of the polite, restrained media representation that had been present at the beginning of the funeral. These people were predatory, focused, and no doubt drawn by the lure of Constantine and the chance to reinvent an old scandal.

The disbelief she'd felt as she'd met Constantine's gaze across her father's grave increased. How dare he come to the funeral? Did he plan to expose them all, most especially her mother, to another media circus?

With an ominous crash of thunder, the rain fell hard, soaking her. Fingers tightening on her purse, she lengthened her stride, breaking into a jog as she rounded the edge of a strip of shade trees that bisected the parking lot. She threw a glance over her shoulder, relieved that the rain had beaten the press back, at least temporarily. A split second later she collided with the solid barrier of a male chest. Constantine.

The hard, muscled imprint of his body burned through the wet silk of her dress as she clutched at a broad set of shoulders.

He jerked his head at a nearby towering oak. "This way. There are more reporters on the other side of the parking lot."

His hand landed in the small of her back. Sienna controlled a small shiver as she felt the heat of his palm, and her heart lurched because she knew Constantine must have followed her with the intent of protecting her. "Thank you."

She appreciated the protection, but that didn't mean she was comfortable with the scenario.

He urged her beneath the shelter of the huge, gnarled oak. The thick, dark canopy of leaves kept the worst of the rain off, but droplets still splashed down, further soaking her hair and the shoulders of her dress.

She found a tissue in her purse and blotted moisture from her face. She didn't bother trying to fix her makeup since there was likely to be very little of it left.

Within moments the rain slackened off and a thin shaft of sunlight penetrated the watery gloom, lighting up the parking lot and the grassy cemetery visible through the trees. Without warning the back of her nose burned and tears trickled down her face. Blindly, she groped for the tissue again.

"Here, use this."

A large square of white linen was thrust into her hand. She sniffed and swallowed a watery, hiccupping sob.

A moment later she found herself wrapped close, her face pressed against Constantine's shoulder, his palm hot against the damp skin at the base of her neck. After a moment of stiffness she gave in and accepted his comfort.

She had cried when she was alone, usually at night and in the privacy of her room so she wouldn't upset her mother, who was still in a state of distressed shock. Most of the time, because she had been so frantically busy she'd managed to contain the grief, but every now and then something set her off.

At some point Constantine loosened his hold enough that she could blow her nose, but it seemed now that she'd started crying, she couldn't stop and the tears kept flowing, although more quietly now. She remained locked in his arms, his palm massaging the hollow between her shoulder blades in a slow, soothing rhythm, the heat from his body driving out the damp chill. Drained by grief, she was happy to just be, and to soak in his hard warmth, the reassurance of his solid male power.

She became aware that the rain had finally stopped, leaving the parking lot wreathed in trailing wisps of steam. In a short while she would pull free and step back, but for the moment her head was thick and throbbing from the crying and she was too exhausted to move.

Constantine's voice rumbled in her ear. "We need to leave. We can't talk here."

She shifted slightly and registered that at some point Constantine had become semi aroused.

For a moment memories crowded her, some blatantly sensual, others laced with hurt and scalding humiliation.

Oh, no, no way. She would not feel this.

Face burning, Sienna jerked free, her purse flying. Shoving wet hair out of her face, she bent to retrieve her purse and the few items that had scattered—lip gloss, compact, car keys.

Her keys. Great idea, because she was leaving now.

If Constantine wanted a conversation he would have to reschedule. There was no way she was staying around for more of the same media humiliation she'd suffered two years ago.

"Damn. Sienna…"

Was that a hint of softness in his eyes? His voice?

No. Couldn't be.

When Constantine crouched down to help gather her things, she hurriedly shoveled the items into her bag. The rain had started up again, an annoying steamy drizzle, although that fact was now inconsequential because every part of her was soaked. Wet hair trailed down her cheeks, her dress felt like it had been glued on and there were puddles in her shoes.

Constantine hadn't fared any better. His gray suit jacket was plastered to his shoulders, his white shirt transparent enough that the bronze color of his skin showed through.

She dragged her gaze from the mesmerizing sight. "Uh-uh. Sorry." She shot to her feet. She was so not talking now. His transparent shirt had reminded her about her dress. It was black, so it wouldn't reveal as much as white fabric when wet, but silk was silk and it was thin. "Your conversation will have to wait. As you can see, I'm wet."

She spun on her heel, looking for an avenue of escape that didn't contain reporters with microphones and cameras.

His arm snaked around her waist, pulling her back against the furnace heat of his body. "After four days of unreturned calls," he growled into her ear, sending a hot shiver down her spine, "if you think I'm going to cool my heels for one more second, you can think again."

Two

Infuriated by the intimacy of his hold and the torrent of unwanted sensation, Sienna pried at Constantine's fingers. "Let. Me. Go."

"No." His gaze slid past hers.

Movement flickered at the periphery of Sienna's vision, she heard a car door slam.

Constantine muttered something curt beneath his breath. Now that the torrential downpour was over, the media were emerging from their vehicles.

He spun her around in his arms. "I wasn't going to do this. You deserve what's coming."

Her head jerked up, catching his jaw and sending a hot flash of pain through her skull, which infuriated her even more. "Like I did last time? Oh, very cool, Constantine. As if I'm some kind of hardened criminal just because I care about my family—"

Something infinitely more dangerous than the threat of

unwanted media exposure stirred in his eyes. "Is that what you call it? Interesting concept."

His level tone burned, more than the edgy heat that had invaded her body, or the castigating guilt that had eaten at her for the past two years. That maybe their split had been all her fault, and not just a convenient quick exit for a wealthy bachelor who had developed cold feet. That maybe she had committed a crime in not revealing how dysfunctional and debt-ridden her family was.

Her jaw tightened. "What did I ever do to truly hurt you, Constantine?"

Grim amusement curved his mouth. "If you're looking for a declaration, you're wasting your breath."

"Don't I know it." She planted her palms on his chest and pushed.

He muttered a low, rough Medinian phrase. "Stay still."

The Medinian language—an Italian dialect with Greek and Arabic influences—growled out in that deep velvet tone, sent a shock of awareness through her along with another hot tingling shiver.

Darn, darn, darn. Why did she have to like that?

Incensed that some crazy part of her was actually turned on by this, she kept up the pressure, her palms flattened against the solid muscle of his chest, maintaining the bare inch of space that existed between them.

An inch that wasn't nearly enough given that explosive contact.

Maybe, just maybe, the press would construe this little tussle as Constantine comforting her instead of an undignified scuffle. "Who called the press?" She stabbed an icy glare at him. "You?"

He gave a short bark of laughter. "*Cara,* I pay people to keep them off."

She warded off another one of those hot little jabs of response. "Don't call me—"

"What?" he said. "Darling? Babe? Sweetheart?"

His long, lean fingers gripped her jaw, trapping her. He bent close enough that anyone watching would assume their embrace was intimate, that he was about to kiss her.

A bittersweet pang went through her. She could see the crystalline depths of his eyes, the tiny beads of water clinging to his long, black lashes, the red mark on his jaw where her head had caught him, and a potent recollection spun her back to the first time they had met, two years ago.

It had been dark but, just like now, it had been raining. Her forward vision impeded by an umbrella, she had jogged from a taxi to the front door of a restaurant when they had collided. That time she had ended up on the wet pavement. Her all-purpose little black dress had been shorter, tighter. Consequently the sexy little side split had torn and her umbrella and one shoe had gone missing in action.

Constantine had apologized and asked if anything was broken. Riveted by the low, sexy timbre of his voice as he had crouched down and fitted the shoe back on her foot, she'd had the dizzying conviction that when she had fallen she had landed in the middle of her favorite fairy tale and Prince Charming had never looked so good. She had replied, "No, of course not."

Although, she had whimsically decided, when he left her heart could be broken.

The pressure of Constantine's grip on her arms zapped her back to the present. A muscle pulsed along the side of his jaw and she was made abruptly aware that, his mystifying anger aside, Constantine was just as disturbed as she.

"*Basta*," he growled. Enough.

Constantine jerked back from the soft curve of Sienna's mouth and the heady desire that, despite all of his efforts, he had never been able to eradicate. "You're wearing the same dress."

"No," she snapped back, informing him that in the confusion of the collision she had been as caught up by the past as he. "That was a cocktail dress."

"It feels the same." Wet and sleek and almost as sensual as her skin.

"Take your hands off me and you won't have to feel a thing."

Her voice was clipped and as cool as chipped ice, but the husky catch in her throat, her inability to entirely meet his gaze, told a different story.

He should let her go. She was clearly shaken. Lucas had been right—on the day of her father's funeral he should show compassion. But despite the demands of common decency, Constantine was unwilling to allow her any leeway at all.

Two years ago Sienna Ambrosi had achieved what no other woman had done. She had fooled him utterly. Touching her now should be repugnant to him. Instead, he was riveted by the fierce challenge in her dark eyes and the soft, utterly feminine shape of her body pressed against his. And drawn to find out exactly how vulnerable she was toward him. "Not until I have what I came for."

Her pupils dilated with shock, and any lingering uncertainty he might have entertained about her involvement in her father's scam evaporated. She was in this up to her elegant neck. The confirmation was unexpectedly depressing.

She blushed. "If it's a discussion you want, it will have to wait. In case you hadn't noticed, we're both wet and this is my father's funeral." She shoved at his chest again.

His hold on her arms tightened reflexively. The sudden full-body contact sent another electrifying shock wave of heat through Constantine, and in that moment the list of what he wanted, and needed, expanded.

Two years ago passion had blindsided him to the point that he had looked past his parents' stormy marital history and the tarnished reputation of the Ambrosi family in an attempt to grasp the mirage. He didn't trust what he had felt then, and he trusted it even less now. But he knew one thing for sure: one night wouldn't be enough.

Sienna threw a glance over her shoulder. "This media craziness is all your fault. If you hadn't turned up, they wouldn't have bothered with us."

"Calm down." Constantine studied the approaching reporters. "And unless you want to be on the six o'clock news, stay with me and keep quiet. I'll do the talking."

The two dark-suited men who had been flanking Constantine earlier materialized and strolled toward the reporters.

In that moment Sienna realized they had been joined by a television crew.

The barrage of questions started. "Ms. Ambrosi, is it true Ambrosi Pearls is facing bankruptcy?"

"Do you have any comment to make about your father allegedly conning money out of Lorenzo Atraeus?"

Several flashes went off, momentarily blinding her. An ultraslim, glamorous redhead darted beneath one of the bodyguard's arms and shoved a mike in her face. Sienna recognized the reporter from one of the major news channels. "Ms. Ambrosi, can you tell us if charges have been brought?"

Shock made Sienna go first hot then cold. "Charges—?"

"Unless you want a defamations suit," Constantine interjected smoothly, "I suggest you withdraw those questions. For the record Ambrosi Pearls and The Atraeus Group are engaged in negotiations over a business deal. Roberto Ambrosi's death has complicated those negotiations. That's all I'm prepared to say."

"Constantine, is this just about business?" The red-headed reporter, who had been maneuvered out of reach by one of the bodyguards, arched a brow, her face vivid and charming. "If a merger of some kind is in the wind, what about a wedding?"

Constantine hurried Sienna toward a sleek black Audi that had slid to a halt just yards away. "No comment."

Lucas climbed out of the driver's seat and tossed the keys over the hood.

Constantine plucked the keys out of midair and opened the passenger-side door. When Sienna realized Constantine meant her to get into the car, with him, she stiffened. "I have my own—"

Constantine leaned close enough that his breath scorched the skin below her ear. "You can come with me or stay. It's your choice. But if you stay you're on your own with the media."

A shudder of horror swept through her. "I'll come."

"In that case I'm going to need your car keys. One of my security team will collect your car and follow us. When we're clear of the press, you can have your little sports car back."

Suspicion flared. "How do you know I have a sports car?"

"Believe me, after the last few days there isn't much I don't know about you and your family."

"Evidently, from the answers you gave the press, you know a lot more than I do." She dug her keys out of her purse and handed them over. As badly as she resented it, Constantine's suggestion made sense. If she had to return to the cemetery to pick up the car later on, it was an easy bet she'd run into more reporters and more questions she wasn't equipped to answer.

Seconds later she was enclosed in the luxurious interior of the Audi, the tinted windows blocking out the media.

She reached for her seat belt. By the time she had it fastened, Constantine was accelerating away from the curb. Cool air from the air-conditioning unit flowed over her, raising gooseflesh on her damp skin.

Nerves strung taut at the intimacy of being enclosed in the cab of the Audi with Constantine, she reached into her purse and found her small traveling box of tissues. Pulling off a handful, she handed them to Constantine.

His gaze briefly connected with hers. "*Grazie.*"

She glanced away, her heart suddenly pounding. Hostilities were, temporarily at least, on hold. "You're welcome."

She pulled off more tissues and began blotting moisture from her face and arms. There was nothing she could do about her hair or her dress, or the fact that the backs of her legs were sticking to the very expensive leather seats.

She glanced in the rearview mirror. Her small sports car was right behind them, followed by the gleaming dark sedan, which contained the second of Constantine's bodyguards and his brothers. "I see you still travel with a SWAT team."

Constantine smoothly negotiated traffic. "They have their uses."

She flashed him a cool look. There was no way she would thank him yet, not when it was clear that Constantine's presence had attracted the press. Until he had showed up, neither she nor any member of her family had been harassed. She studied the clean line of his profile, the inky crescents of his lashes and the small scar high on one cheekbone. Unbidden, memories flickered—the dark bronze of his skin glowing in the morning light, the habit he'd had of sprawling across her bed, sheets twined around his hips, all long limbs and sleek muscle.

Hot color flooded her cheeks. Hastily she transferred her gaze to the traffic flowing around them. "Now that we're alone you can tell me what that media assault was all about." The very fact that Constantine had interceded on her behalf meant something was very wrong. "Conned? Charges? And what was that about negotiating a deal?"

With her background in commercial law, Sienna was Ambrosi Pearls' legal counsel. At no point in the past two years had her father so much as mentioned The Atraeus Group, or any financial dealings. After the loan Roberto had tried to negotiate had fallen through, along with her engagement, the subject had literally been taboo.

Constantine braked for a set of lights. "There is a problem, but I'm not prepared to discuss it while I'm driving."

While they waited in traffic her frustration mounted. "If you won't discuss it…" her fingers sketched quotation marks in the air, "then at least tell me why, if Ambrosi Pearls is supposed to have done something so wrong, you're helping me instead of throwing me to the media wolves?"

"In an instant replay of the way I treated you two years ago?"

The silky edge to his voice made her tense. "Yes."

The lights turned green. Constantine accelerated through the intersection. "Because you're in shock, and you've just lost your father."

Something about the calmness of his manner sent a prickle of unease down her spine, sharpened all of her senses.

His ruthless business reputation aside, Constantine was known to be a philanthropist with a compassionate streak. He frequently gave massive sums to charities, but that compassion had never been directed toward either her or her family.

"I don't believe you. There's something else going on." During the short conversation during which he had broken their engagement, Sienna had tried to make him understand the complications of her father's skyrocketing gambling debts and the struggle she had simply to support her mother and keep Ambrosi Pearls afloat. That in the few stressful days she'd had before Constantine had discovered the deal, the logic of her father asking Lorenzo Atraeus for a loan had seemed viable.

She had wasted her breath.

Constantine had been too busy walking out the door to listen to the painful details of her family's financial struggle.

"As you heard from the reporters, there is very definitely 'something else going on.' If you'll recall, that was the reason our engagement ended."

"My father proposed a business deal that your father wanted."

"Reestablishing a pearl facility on Medinos was a proposal based on opportunism and nostalgia, not profit."

Her anger flared at the opportunism crack. "And the bottom line is so much more important to you than honoring the past or creating something beautiful."

"Farming pretty baubles in a prime coastal location slated for development as a resort didn't make business sense then and it makes no sense now. The Atraeus Group has more lucrative business options than restoring Medinos's pearl industry."

"Options that don't require any kind of history or sentiment. Like mining gold and building luxury hotels."

His gaze briefly captured hers. "I don't recall that you

ever had any problem with the concept of making money. As I remember it, two years ago money came before 'sentiment.'"

Sienna controlled the rush of guilty heat to her cheeks "I refuse to apologize for a business deal I didn't instigate.' Or for being weak enough to have felt an overwhelming relief that, finally, there could be an answer to her family's crippling financial problems. "My only sin was not having the courage to tell you about the deal."

She stared out of the passenger-side window as Constantine turned into the parking lot of a shopping mall. It was too late now to admit that she had been afraid the impending disgrace of her father's gambling and financial problems would harm their engagement.

As it turned out, the very thing she had feared had happened. Constantine believed she had broken his trust, that her primary interest in him had always been monetary. "I apologized for not discussing the deal with you," she said, hating the husky note in her voice, "but, quite frankly, that was something I would have assumed your father would have done."

Constantine slotted the Audi into a space. She heard the snick as he released his seat belt. He turned in his seat and rested an arm along the back of hers, making her even more suffocatingly aware of his presence.

"Even knowing that my father's lack of transparency indicated he was keeping the deal under wraps?"

A dark sedan slid into a space beside the Audi. One of Constantine's bodyguards, with Lucas in the passenger seat and Zane in the rear. A flash of cream informed her that her sports car, driven by the second bodyguard, had just been parked in an adjacent space.

Feeling hemmed in by overlarge Medinian males, Sienna released her seat belt and reached for her purse. "I didn't understand that you were so against the idea of re-establishing a pearl industry on Medinos."

Stupidly, when she hadn't been frightened that she would lose Constantine and burying her head in the sand, she had been too busy coping with the hectic media pressure their engagement had instigated.

Life in a fish tank hadn't been fun.

"Just as I couldn't understand why you failed to discuss the agreement, which just happened to have been drawn up the day following our engagement announcement."

Her gaze snapped to his. "How many times do I have to say it? I had nothing to do with the loan. Think about it, Constantine. If I was that grasping and devious I would have waited until after we were married."

A tense silence stretched, thickened. Now she really couldn't breathe. Fumbling at the car door, she pushed it wide.

Constantine leaned across and hauled the door shut, pinning Sienna in place before she could scramble out. The uncharacteristic surge of temper that flowed through him at the deliberate taunt was fueled by the physical frustration that had been eating at him ever since he had decided he had to see her again.

The question of just why he had taken one look at Sienna two years ago and fallen in instant lust, he decided, no longer existed. It had ceased to be the instant he had glimpsed her silky blond head at the funeral. Even wet and bedraggled, her eyes red-rimmed from crying, Sienna was gorgeous in a fragile, exotic way that hooked into every male instinct he possessed.

The combination of delicacy paired with sensuality, in Anglo-Saxon terms, was crazy-making. He was at once caught between the desire to protect and cushion her from the slightest upset and the desire to take her to bed and make love to her until she surrendered utterly.

It was an unsettling fact that he would rather argue with Sienna than spend time with any other woman, no matter how gorgeous or focused on pleasing him she might be.

"Now that's interesting. I assumed that the reason you stayed quiet about the loan was that your father needed the money too badly to wait."

Her face went bone-white and he knew in that instant that he had gone too far.

Then, hot color burned along her cheekbones and the aura of haunted fragility evaporated. "Or maybe I was simply following orders?"

His gaze shifted to her pale mouth, the line of her throat as she swallowed. "No," he said flatly.

Sienna had been Roberto's precocious second-in-command for the past four years. She had run the family's pearl house with consummate skill and focused ambition while her father had steadily gambled the profits away at various casinos. The last time she had taken an order from Roberto, she had been in the cradle. If she had a weakness, it was that she needed money.

His money.

And she still did.

She pulled in a jerky breath. He felt the rise and fall of her breasts against his arm, the feathery warmth along his jaw as she exhaled. The light, evocative scent she wore teased his nostrils as flash after flash of memory turned the air molten.

A tap on the passenger-side window broke the tension. One of his security guards.

Constantine released his hold on the door handle, his temper tightly controlled as he watched Sienna climb out and collect her car keys.

Levering himself out of the Audi into the now blistering heat of early afternoon, Constantine gave the guard his instructions. For the past four days he had seldom been without an escort but for the next hour he required absolute privacy.

Peeling out of his damp jacket, he tossed it behind the driver's seat. He frowned as he noticed Lucas speaking with Sienna. From the brevity of the exchange he was aware that his brother had simply offered his condolences, but Sienna's smile evoked an unsettling response.

The fact that Lucas was every inch a dangerous Atraeus male shouldn't register, but after the charged few moments in the Audi, the knowledge of just how successful his brother was with women was distinctly unpalatable.

Constantine strolled toward Sienna as she slid her cell phone out of her purse and answered a call.

Lucas waylaid him with a brief jerk of his chin. "Are you sure you know what you're doing?"

"Positive."

"It didn't look like a business discussion back at the cemetery, and it sure as hell didn't look like a business discussion just then."

Constantine knew his gaze was cold enough to freeze. "Just as long as you remember that Sienna Ambrosi is my business."

Lucas lifted a brow. "Message received."

Jaw tight, Constantine watched as Lucas climbed into the passenger-side seat of the dark sedan. He lifted a hand as the car cruised out of the parking lot. Maybe he hadn't needed to warn Lucas off, but the instinct to do so had been knee-jerk and primitive. In that moment he had acknowledged one clear fact: for the foreseeable future, until he had gotten her out of his system, Sienna Ambrosi was his.

While he waited for Sienna to terminate her call, he grimly considered that fact, sifting through every nuance of the past hour. The tension that had gripped him from the moment he had laid eyes on Sienna at the funeral tightened another notch.

Constantine knew his own nature. He was focused, single-minded. When he fixed on a goal he achieved it. His absolute commitment to running the family business was both a necessity and a passion and he had never flinched from making hard choices. Two years ago, severing all connection with Sienna and the once pampered and aristocratic Ambrosi family had been one of those choices.

Sliding dark glasses onto the bridge of his nose, Constantine crossed his arms over his chest and studied the pure line of Sienna's profile, the luscious combination of creamy skin and dark eyes, her soft pale mouth.

Until he had been handed an investigative report he had commissioned on Ambrosi Pearls and had discovered that Sienna had been linked on at least three occasions with Alex Panopoulos, a wealthy retailer.

He still remembered the moment of disorientation, the grim fury when he'd considered that Panopoulos could be Sienna's lover.

He had soon eliminated that scenario.

According to the very efficient private eye employed by the security firm, Panopoulos was actively hunting but the Greek hadn't yet managed to snare either of the Ambrosi girls.

Sienna registered Constantine's impatience as she ended her conversation with Carla, who had been concerned that she had been caught up in the media frenzy in the parking lot.

Constantine lifted a brow. "Where do we talk? Your place or mine?"

Sienna dropped her phone back into her purse. After the tense moments in the car and the sensual shock of Constantine invading her space, she couldn't hide her dismay at the thought of Constantine's apartment. Two years ago they had spent a lot of time there. It had also been the scene of their breakup.

The thought of Constantine in the sanctuary of her own small place was equally unacceptable. "Not the apartments."

"I don't have the apartment anymore. I own a house along the coast."

"I thought you liked living in town."

"I changed my mind."

Just like he had about her. Instantly and unequivocally.

He opened the door of her small soft-top convertible. Feeling as edgy as a cat, her stomach tight with nerves, she slipped into the driver's seat, carefully avoiding any physical contact. "Carla's taken Mom to a family lunch at Aunt Via's apartment, so they'll be occupied for the next couple of hours. I can meet you at my parent's beach house at Pier Point. That's where I've been staying since Dad died."

Constantine closed her door. Bracing his hands on the window frame, he leaned down, maintaining eye contact. "That explains why you haven't been at your apartment, although not why you haven't been returning my calls at work."

"If you wanted to get hold of me that badly you should have rung my mother."

"I got through twice," he said grimly. "Both times I got Carla."

Sienna could feel her cheeks heating. After Sienna's breakup with Constantine, Carla had become fiercely protective. Constantine hadn't gotten through, because Carla would have made it her mission to stop him.

"Sorry about that," she said, without any trace of sympathy in her voice. "Carla said there had been a couple of crank calls, then the press started bothering Mom in the evenings, so we went to stay at the beach house."

Constantine had also left a number of messages at work, which, when she had been in the office at all, Sienna had ignored. She had been feverishly trying to unravel her father's twisted affairs. Calling Constantine had ranked right up there with chatting to disgruntled creditors or having a cozy discussion with IRD about the payments Ambrosi Pearls had failed to make.

"If Pier Point is hostile territory, maybe we should meet on neutral ground?"

Was that a hint of amusement in his voice?

No, whatever it was Constantine was feeling, it wasn't amusement. There had been a definite predatory edge to him. She had seen a liquid silver flash of it at the gravesite, then been burned by it again in the parking lot.

The foreboding that had gripped her at the cemetery returned, playing havoc with her pulse again.

Suddenly shaky with a combination of exhaustion and nerves, she started the car and busied herself with fastening her seat belt. "The beach house is far enough out of town that the press isn't likely to be staking it out. If this conversation is taking the direction I think it is, we'd better meet there."

"Tell me," he said curtly. "What direction, exactly, do you think this conversation will take?"

"A conversation with Constantine Atraeus?" Her smile was as tightly strung as her nerves. "Now let me see... Two options—sex or money. Since it can't possibly be sex, my vote's on the money."

Three

Money was the burning agenda, but as Sienna drove into Pier Point, with Constantine following close enough behind to make her feel herded, she wasn't entirely sure about the sex.

Earlier, in the Audi, Constantine's muscular heat engulfing her, she had been sharply aware of his sexual intent. He had wanted her and he hadn't been shy about letting her know. The moment had been underscored by an unnerving flash of déjà vu.

The first time Constantine had kissed her had been in his car. He had cupped her chin and lowered his mouth to hers, and despite her determination to keep her distance, she had wound her arms around his neck, angled her jaw and leaned into the kiss. Even though she had only known him for a few hours she had been swept off her feet. She hadn't been able to resist him, and he had known it.

Shaking off the too-vivid recollection, she signaled and

turned her small sports car into her mother's driveway. Barely an hour after the unpleasant clash across her father's grave, those kinds of memories shouldn't register. The fact that Constantine wanted her meant little more than that he was a man with a normal, healthy libido. In the past two years he had been linked with a number of wealthy, beautiful women, each one a serious contender for the position of Mrs. Constantine Atraeus.

He turned into the driveway directly behind her. As Sienna accelerated up the small, steep curve, the sense of being pursued increased. She used her remote to close the electronic gates at the bottom of the drive, just in case the press had followed. After parking, she grabbed her handbag and walked across the paved courtyard that fronted the old cliff-top house.

Constantine was already out of his car. She noticed that in the interim he'd rolled his sleeves up, baring tanned, muscled forearms. She unlocked the front door and as he loomed over her in the bare, sun-washed hall, her stomach, already tense, did another annoying little flip.

He indicated she precede him. She couldn't fault his manners, but that didn't change the fact that with Constantine padding behind her like a large, hunting cat, she felt like prey.

"What happened to the furniture?"

The foreign intonation in his deep voice set her on edge all over again. Suddenly, business agenda or not, it seemed unbearably intimate to be alone with him in the quiet stillness of the almost empty house.

Sienna skimmed blank walls that had once held a collection of paintings, including an exquisitely rendered Degas. "Sold, along with all the valuable artwork my grandfather collected."

She threw him a tight smile. "Auctioned, along with

every piece of real jewelry Mom, Carla and I owned—including the pearls. Now isn't that a joke? We own a pearl house, but we can't afford our own products."

She pushed open the ornate double doors to her father's study and stood aside as Constantine walked into the room, which held only a desk and a couple of chairs.

His gaze skimmed bare floorboards and the ranks of empty built-in mahogany bookshelves, which had once housed a rare book collection. She logged the moment he finally comprehended what a sham their lives had become. They sold pearls to the wealthy and projected sleek, rich-list prosperity for the sake of the company, but the struggle had emptied them out, leaving her mother, Carla and herself with nothing.

He surveyed the marks on the wall that indicated paintings had once hung there and the dangling ceiling fitting that had once held a chandelier. "What didn't he sell to pay gambling debts?"

For a split second Sienna thought Constantine was taking a cheap shot, implying that both she and Carla had been up for auction, but she dismissed the notion. When he had broken their engagement his reasons had been clear-cut. After her father's failed deal he had made it plain he could no longer trust her or the connection with her family. His stand had been tough and uncompromising, because he hadn't allowed her a defense, but he had never at any time been malicious.

"We still have the house, and we've managed to keep the business running. It's not much, but it's a start. Ambrosi employs over one hundred people, some of whom have worked for us for decades. When it came down to keeping those people in work, selling possessions and family heirlooms wasn't a difficult choice."

Although she didn't expect Constantine with his reputation for being coldly ruthless in business to agree. "Wait here," she said stiffly, "I'll get towels."

Glad for a respite, she walked upstairs to her room. With swift movements she peeled off her ruined shoes, changed them for dry ones then checked her appearance in the dresser mirror. A small shock went through her when she noted the glitter of her eyes and the warm flush on her cheeks. With her creased dress and tousled hair, the look was disturbingly sensual.

Walking through to the bathroom, she towel-dried her hair, combed it and decided not to bother changing the dress, which was almost dry. She shouldn't care whether Constantine thought she was attractive or not, and if she did, she needed to squash the notion. The sooner this conversation was over and he was gone, the better.

She collected a fresh towel from the linen closet and walked back downstairs.

Constantine turned from the breathtaking view of the Pacific Ocean as she entered the study, his light gaze locking briefly with hers.

Breath hitching at the sudden pounding of her heart, Sienna handed him the towel, taking care not to let their fingers brush. She indicated the view. "One of the few assets we haven't yet had to sell, but only because Mom sold the town house this week. Although this place is mortgaged to the hilt."

It would go, too. It was only a matter of time.

He ran the towel briefly over his hair before tossing it over the arm of a chair. "I didn't know things had gotten this bad."

But, she realized, he had known her father's gambling had gotten out of hand. "Why should you? Ambrosi Pearls has nothing to do with either Medinos or The Atraeus Group."

His expression didn't alter, but suddenly any trace of compassion was gone. Good. Relief unfolded inside her. If anything could kill the skittish knowledge that not only was she on edge, she was sexually on edge, a straightforward business discussion would do it.

She indicated that Constantine take a seat and walked around to stand behind her father's desk, underlining her role as Ambrosi Pearls' CEO. "Not many people know the company's financial position, and I would appreciate if you wouldn't spread it around. With the papers speculating about losses, I'm having a tough time convincing some of our customers that Ambrosi is solid."

Constantine ignored the chair in favor of standing directly opposite her, arms crossed over his chest, neutralizing her attempt at dominance.

Sienna averted her gaze from the way the damp fabric of his shirt clung to his shoulders, the sleek aura of male power that swirled around Constantine Atraeus like a cloak.

"It must have been difficult, trying to run a business with a gambler at the helm."

As abruptly as if an internal switch had been thrown, Sienna's temper boiled over. Finally, the issue he hadn't wanted to talk about two years ago. "I don't think you can understand at all. Did your father gamble?"

Constantine's gaze narrowed. "Only in a good way."

"Of course." Lorenzo Atraeus had been an excellent businessman. "With good information and solid investment backing so he could make money, then more money. Unlike my father who consistently found ways to lose it, both in business and at the blackjack table." Her heart was pounding; her blood pressure was probably off the register. "You don't know what it's like to lose and keep on losing because you can't control someone in your family."

"My family has some experience with loss."

His expression was grim, his tone remote, reminding her that the Atraeus family had lived in poverty on Medinos for years, farming goats. Constantine's grandfather had even worked for hers, until the Ambrosis had lost their original pearl business when it had been bombed during the war. But that had all been years ago. This was now.

She leaned forward, every muscle taut. "Running a business with a gambler at the helm hasn't been easy."

He spread his palms on the desk and suddenly they were nose to nose. "If it got that bad why didn't you get out?"

And suddenly, the past was alive between them and she was taking a weird, giddy delight in fighting with Constantine. Maybe it was a reaction, a backlash to the grief and strain of the funeral, or the simple fact that she was sick of clamping down on her emotions and tired of hiding the truth. "And abandon my family and all the people who depend on our company for their livelihood?" She smiled tightly. "It was never an option, and I hope I never arrive at that point. Which brings us to the conversation you want so badly. How much do we owe?"

"Did you know that two months ago your father paid a visit to Medinos?"

Shock held her immobile. "No."

"Are you aware that he had plans to start up a pearl industry there?"

"Not possible." But blunt denial didn't ease the cold dread forming in her stomach. "We barely have enough capital to operate in Sydney." Her father had driven what had been a thriving business into the ground. "We're in no position to expand."

Something shifted in Constantine's gaze, and for a

fleeting second she had a sense that, like it or not, he had reached some kind of decision.

Constantine indicated a document he must have dropped on the desk while she'd been out of the room. Sienna studied the thick parchment. Her knees wobbled. A split second later she was sitting in her father's old leather chair, fighting disbelief as she skimmed the text.

Not one loan but several. She had expected the first loan to date back to the first large deposit she had found in her father's personal account several weeks ago, and she wasn't disappointed.

She lifted her head to find Constantine still watching her. "Why did Lorenzo lend anything to my father? He knew he had a gambling problem."

"My father was terminally ill and clearly not in his right mind. When he died a month ago, we knew there was a deficit. Unfortunately, the documents confirming the loans to your father weren't located until five days ago."

Her jaw clenched. "Why didn't you stop him?"

"Believe me, if I had been there I would have, but I was out of the country at the time. To compound the issue, he bypassed the usual channels and retained an old friend, his retired legal counsel, to draw up the contracts."

Constantine ran his fingers around his nape, his expression abruptly impatient. "I see you're now beginning to understand the situation. Your father has been running Ambrosi Pearls and his gambling addiction on The Atraeus Group's money. An amount he 'borrowed' from a dying man on the basis of a business he had no intention of setting up."

Fraud.

Now the questions fired at her by the reporters made sense. "Is that what you told the press?"

"I think you know me better than that."

She felt oddly relieved. It shouldn't matter that Constantine hadn't been the one who had leaked the story, but it did.

Someone, most likely an employee, would have sold the information to the press.

Sienna stared at the figure involved and felt her normal steely optimism and careful plans for Ambrosi Pearls dissolve.

Firming her chin, she stared out at the bright blue summer sky and the endless, hazy vista of the Pacific Ocean, and tried to regroup. There had to be a way out of this; she had wrangled the company out of plenty of tight spots before. All she had to do was think.

Small, disparate pieces of information clicked into place. Constantine not wanting to talk to her at the funeral or in the car, the way he had remained standing while she had read through the documents.

He had wanted to watch her reaction when she read the paperwork.

Her gaze snapped to his. "You thought I was part of this."

Constantine's expression didn't alter.

Something in her plummeted. Sienna pushed to her feet. The loan documents cascaded to the floor; she barely noticed them. When Lorenzo Atraeus had died, he had left an enormous fortune based on a fabulously rich gold mine and a glittering retail and hotel empire to his three sons, Constantine, Lucas and Zane.

It shouldn't be uppermost in her mind, but it suddenly struck her that if Ambrosi Pearls was in debt to The

Atraeus Group, by definition—as majority shareholder—
that meant Constantine.

Constantine's gaze was oddly bleak. "Now you're getting it. Unless you can come up with the money, I now own
Ambrosi Pearls lock, stock and barrel."

Four

The vibration of a cell phone broke the electrifying silence.

Constantine answered the call, relieved at the sudden release of tension, the excuse to step back from a situation that had spiraled out of control.

He had practically threatened Sienna, a tactic he had never before resorted to, even when dealing with slick, professional fraudsters. In light of the heart-pounding discovery that Sienna hadn't known about her father's latest scam, his behavior was inexcusable. He should have stepped back, reassessed, postponed the meeting.

Gotten a grip before he wrecked any chance that she might want him again.

Unfortunately, Sienna doing battle with him across the polished width of her father's desk had put a kink in his strategy. Her cheeks had been flushed, her eyes fiery, shunting him back in time to hot, sultry nights and tangled sheets. It was hard to think tactically when all he wanted to do was kiss her.

She had never been this animated or passionate with him before, he realized. Even in bed he had always been grimly aware that she was holding back, that there was a part of her he couldn't reach.

That she was more committed to Ambrosi Pearls than she had ever been to him.

To compound the problem, he had mentioned the bad old days when the Atraeus family had been dirt-poor. Given that he wanted Sienna back in his bed, the last thing he needed was for her to view him as the grandson of the gardener.

Jaw tight, he turned to stare out at the sea view as he spoke to his personal assistant. Tomas had been trying to reach him for the past hour. Constantine had been aware he had missed calls, something he seldom did, but for once, business hadn't been first priority.

Another uncharacteristic lapse.

Constantine hung up and broodingly surveyed Sienna as she gathered the pages she had knocked onto the floor and stacked them in a precise pile on the desktop. Even with her dress crumpled and her makeup gone, she looked elegant and classy, the quintessential lady.

A car door slammed somewhere in the distance. The staccato of high heels on the walkway was followed by the sound of the front door opening.

Constantine caught the flare of desperation in Sienna's gaze. Witnessing that moment of sheer panic was like a kick in the chest. He was here to right a wrong that had been done to his father, but Sienna was also trying to protect her family, most specifically her mother, from him. It was a sobering moment. "Don't worry," he said quietly. "I won't tell her."

Sienna stifled a surge of relief and just had time to send Constantine a grateful glance before Margaret Ambrosi stepped into the room, closely followed by Carla.

"What's going on?" her mother demanded in the cool, clear tone that had gotten her through thirty years with a husband who had given her more heartache than joy. "And don't try to fob me off, because I know something's wrong."

"Mrs. Ambrosi." Constantine used a tone that was far gentler than any Sienna could ever remember him using with her. "My condolences. Sienna and I were just discussing the details of a business deal your husband initiated a few months ago."

Carla's jaw was set. "I don't believe Dad would have transacted anything without—"

Margaret Ambrosi's hand stayed her. "So that's why Roberto made the trip to Europe. I should have known."

Carla frowned. "He went to Paris and Frankfurt. He didn't go near the Mediterranean."

An emotion close to anger momentarily replaced the exhaustion etched on her mother's face.

"Roberto left a day earlier because he wanted to stop off at Medinos first. He said he wanted to visit the site of the old pearl facility and find his grandparents' graves. If anything should have warned me he was up to something that should have been it. Roberto didn't have a sentimental bone in his body. He went to Medinos on business."

"That's correct," Constantine said in the same gentle tone, and despite the antagonism and the towering issue of the debt, Sienna could have hugged him.

One of the qualities that had made her fall so hard for Constantine two years ago had been the way he was with his family. Put simply, he loved and protected them with the kind of fierce loyalty that still had the power to send a shiver down her spine. After years of coping with a father who had always put himself first, the prospect of being included in Constantine's family circle, of being the focus of that fierce protective instinct, had been utterly seductive.

That had been the prime reason she had frozen inside when she had found out that her father had done an under-the-table deal with Roberto Atraeus. She hadn't been able to discuss it; she had been afraid to even think about it. She had known how Constantine would react and when the details of the loan had surfaced, the very thing she had feared most had happened. He had shut her out.

She blinked, snapping herself out of a memory that still had the power to hurt.

Constantine checked his watch. "If you'll excuse me, I have another appointment. Once again, my apologies for intruding on your grief."

His cool gray eyes connected with hers, the message clear. They hadn't finished their discussion.

"I'll see you out." Shoving the loan documents out of sight in a drawer, she followed Constantine out into the bare hallway. As much as she didn't want to spend any more time with him, she did want to get him out of the house and away from her mother before she realized there was a problem.

The bright sunlight shafting through the open front door was glaring after the dim coolness of the study.

"Watch your step."

Constantine's hand cupped her elbow, the gesture nothing more than courtesy, but enough to reignite the humming awareness and the antagonism that had been so useful in getting her through the last hour and a half.

Pulse pounding, she lengthened her stride, moving away from the tingling heat of his touch and her growing conviction that Constantine wasn't entirely unhappy with the power he now wielded over Ambrosi Pearls, and her. That behind the business-speak simmered a very personal agenda.

Her stomach tightened at the thought, her mouth going dry as the taut moments in his car replayed themselves. Barely two hours ago Constantine Atraeus, the man, hadn't registered on her awareness. She had blanked him out, along with everything else that was not directly involved with either Ambrosi Pearls or her father's funeral arrangements. Now she couldn't seem to stop the hot flashes of memory and an acute awareness of him. "Thank you for not saying anything about the debt to Mom."

"If I'd thought your mother was involved, I would have mentioned it."

"Which means you do think I'm involved."

Suddenly the whole idea that she could be crazily attracted to Constantine again was so not an issue.

Constantine followed her out into the courtyard and depressed the Audi's key. The sleek car unlocked with an expensive thunk. "You've been running Ambrosi single-handedly for the past eighteen months. And paying Roberto's debts."

She grabbed a remote control from her car and opened the gate at the bottom of the driveway. As far as she was concerned, the sooner he left the better. "By selling family assets, not trying to take more loans when we're already overcommitted."

Constantine's phone buzzed. He picked up the call and spoke briefly in Medinian. She heard Lucas's name and mention of the company lawyer, Ben Vitalis. Business. That explained all three Atraeus brothers being in Sydney at the same time, no matter for how short a period. It also emphasized the fact that Constantine might be here to deal with the mess her father had entangled them both in, but on The Atraeus Group's global radar, Ambrosi Pearls was only a blip.

The tension that gripped her stomach and chest tightened another notch. Which, once again, pointed to the personal agenda.

Constantine terminated the call. "We have a lot to discuss, but the discussion will have to wait until tonight. I'll send a car for you at eight. We can talk over dinner."

She stiffened. Dinner definitely sounded more personal than business, which didn't make sense.

He had been gone for two years. In that time he hadn't ever contacted her. For the first couple of months, she had waited for him to call or to turn up on her doorstep and say he was sorry and that he wanted to try again. The fact that he never had had been an unexpected gift.

She had gotten over him. If he thought she was going to jump feetfirst into some kind of affair with him now, he could think again. "In case you didn't notice, I buried my father today. We have to talk, but I need a couple of days."

Which would give her time to consult their accountant and investigate options. The chance that she could either raise the loan money or make a big sale that quickly was slim, but she had to try. It would also give her time to step back from the mystifying knee-jerk reactions she kept having toward Constantine. She no longer loved him and she certainly did not like him. She could not want him.

Constantine opened the car door. "A few days ago that could have been arranged, but you chose to avoid me. I'm flying out at midnight tomorrow. If you can't find time before then, tomorrow there's a cocktail party at my house, a business meet and greet for The Atraeus Group's retail partners."

"No." As imperative as it was to come to grips with the looming financial disaster, the last thing she wanted was to attend a reception with Constantine, informal or not, at his house. "We'll have to reschedule. In any case I would prefer to talk during business hours."

In a neutral, business setting where the male/female dynamic could be neatly contained.

The businesslike gleam in Sienna's gaze sent irritation flashing through Constantine.

None of this was going as he had envisioned. Not only did he feel like a villain, but she was now trying to call the shots and he was on the verge of losing his temper again, something else that never happened. "We need to talk. When is the reading of the will scheduled?"

"This afternoon, at four."

He saw the moment the reality of her position sank in. If she didn't agree to a meeting he could conceivably send a representative to the reading of the will with the loan documents. It was something he had no intention of doing, specifically because it would frighten her mother.

"You're out of options, Sienna." Constantine slid behind the wheel of the Audi before he caved and started hemorrhaging options that would leave him out of her life altogether.

The engine started with a throaty purr. "Be ready tomorrow at eight."

The following morning, Constantine walked into The Atraeus Group's Sydney office. He was ten minutes late, not quite a first, but close. He had been late once before; two years ago to be exact.

Lucas and Zane, who were both gym freaks, were already there, looking sharp and energized against the clinical backdrop of chrome and leather furniture and executive gray walls. Constantine preferred to jog on the beach or swim rather than subject himself to a rigid workout program. Watching the sunrise and getting sand in his cross trainers was the one break he cut himself in a day that was already too regimented. After a near sleepless night spent pacing, however, this morning he had figured he could forgo his normal dawn run.

He zeroed in on the take-out coffee sitting on his desk and frowned in the direction of his brothers who were both regarding him with the kind of interested gaze that made him wonder if he'd grown an extra head or put his shirt on backward. "What?"

Zane ducked his head and stared hard at the glossy business magazine he was reading, which was odd in itself. His usual reading material involved fast boats, even faster cars and art installations that Constantine didn't pretend to understand. Lucas, meanwhile, hummed snatches of something vaguely familiar under his breath.

His temper now definitely on a short fuse, Constantine drank a mouthful of the coffee, which was lukewarm.

Lucas dropped a section of the morning paper on his desk. "Now that you've had some caffeine you'd better take a look at this."

Even though he had expected it, the photo taken at Roberto Ambrosi's funeral took his breath away. He remembered holding Sienna so she wouldn't walk into the barrage of cameras, but the clinch the reporter had snapped didn't look anything like protective restraint. His gaze was fused with hers, and he looked like he was about to kiss her. From memory, that was exactly how he had felt.

He skimmed the short article, going still inside when he read the statement that he had arrived in Sydney the day before Roberto Ambrosi had dropped dead from a heart attack for the specific purpose of arranging a meeting with the head of Ambrosi Pearls.

The article, thankfully, didn't go so far as to say he had

caused Ambrosi's fatal heart attack, but it did claim a wedding announcement was expected. The tune Lucas had been humming was suddenly recognizable; it had been the *Wedding March*.

He cursed softly. "When I find out who leaked the story to the press—"

"You'll what?" Lucas crumpled his own empty take-out cup and tossed it in the trash bin. "Give them a pay raise?"

Constantine dropped the newspaper on his desk. "Is it that obvious?"

"You're here."

Zane pushed to his feet, the movement fluid. "If you want to step back from the negotiations, Lucas and I can delay the New Zealand trip. Better still, let Vitalis handle the loan."

"No." Constantine's reply was knee-jerk, his gaze suddenly cold enough to freeze, despite the fact that he knew both Lucas and Zane were only trying to protect him.

Zane shrugged, his shoulders broad in his designer jacket. "Your choice, but if you stay in Sydney the press is going to have a field day."

Constantine studied the grainy newspaper photo again. "I can handle it. In any case I'm flying out tomorrow night."

A cell phone vibrated. Lucas's expression was grim as he took his phone out of his pocket. "The sooner the better. You don't need this."

Jaw tense, Constantine stalked over to the glass panels that took up one entire wall of his office, drinking his coffee while Lucas answered his cell.

From here he could see one corner of the Ambrosi building. The office block, dwarfed as it was by the skyscrapers that sprouted near the heart of the Central Business District, clearly undercapitalized one of the more valuable pieces of real estate in town.

Although the monetary value of anything Ambrosi was fast ceasing to hold any meaning for him.

He couldn't stop thinking about the way Sienna had tried to protect her mother yesterday. If she had read the newspaper story, she would hold an even worse opinion of him now, despite the fact that in his own way he had been trying to help her family by keeping the location of her father's heart attack quiet. The furor of Roberto dropping dead in a casino would not help the grieving family or do Ambrosi Pearls any favors.

Not that Sienna was likely to attribute any honorable motivations to his actions.

Lucas terminated his call. "That was one of our security guys. Apparently a news crew has found the location of the Pier Point house. Sienna's down on the beach sunbathing."

Constantine went cold inside. "They must have followed me yesterday." He dropped his now empty take-out cup in the trash.

This morning's story had been buried in the social pages of the paper. If he wasn't fast enough, Sienna could be a lead story by tomorrow morning.

In Sienna's eyes, he was certain that somehow, that, also, would be his fault.

Lucas looked concerned. "Do you want company?"

Constantine barely spared Lucas and Zane a glance. "Catch your flight out. Like I said, I can handle this."

Five

Sienna saw the reporter while he was negotiating the narrow track down to the tiny bay below the Pier Point house. Annoyance flashed through her at the intrusion, and the realization that the reporters had found her family hideaway. No surprises how that had happened, she thought grimly.

To leave the beach she would either have to swim out or climb past the reporter, which meant he would be snapping pictures of her in a bikini all the way. Not good.

She jogged into the water. A leisurely swim later, she pulled herself up onto a small diving pontoon anchored out in the bay.

Slicking wet hair back from her face, she checked out the reporter who was now standing with a forlorn air at the edge of the water. Satisfied that he didn't have a telescopic lens, because if he did he would have had it trained on her by now, Sienna sat down on the bobbing platform and waited for him to leave. If necessary, she could swim to the other end of the bay, climb the rocky slope and walk back to the house.

Long minutes ticked by. She checked her waterproof watch. If he decided to wait her out on the beach, she would have to consider the swim because she was expecting a call in just under an hour back at the house.

She lay down on her back, making herself an even smaller target for the reporter's lens, and forced herself to relax. All last night her stomach churned from the discovery she'd made the previous afternoon that Constantine had been in town when her father had died.

She had spent the night tossing and turning, alternately furious with Constantine because he seemed to be at the center of her entire financial mess, then paralyzed with fear because there didn't seem to be a thing she could do to stop him from taking everything.

As satisfying as it would be to blame Constantine, though, she knew that wasn't fair. Her father, who had been a charming, larger-than-life rogue, had had a number of minor heart attacks over the years. Just recently he had been scheduled for a bypass operation, because his health had gone rapidly downhill. His doctor had specifically told him to stay away from casinos because the stress and excitement were detrimental to his health.

She shielded her eyes from the sun with the back of her hand and smothered a yawn. She allowed her lids to close, just for a few seconds. When she opened them, she was abruptly aware that more than a few seconds had passed.

Cautiously, she scanned the beach, which was empty. The sound that had jerked her out of sleep suddenly fell into its correct context. It wasn't the rhythmic splash of waves against the pontoon. A swimmer, large, male and muscular, was cutting through the water, heading straight for her.

It wasn't the reporter, who appeared to have left the beach. She recognized that smooth, effortless crawl. It was Constantine.

Slipping into the water, she struck out away from the pontoon. If she swam in a semicircle she would be able to avoid Constantine and hopefully get back to the beach before he did. With any luck he would stay aimed at the pontoon and wouldn't realize that she had gone.

Maybe the fight-or-flight reaction was overkill, but dressed in a skimpy pink bikini she preferred to go with the unreasoning panic. If she was going to talk to a mostly naked and wet Constantine, she wanted to be wearing clothes.

Turning her head as she swam, she checked out the pontoon and saw Constantine swimming directly behind her. Her heart pounded out of control. She was good in the water, but Constantine was a whole lot better. When they had been dating he had encouraged her to take a scuba diving course because he had wanted her to share his passion for the sport. After she had qualified he had taken her out a couple of times before they had broken up, making sure she was water fit and proficient with the complex array of scuba gear. She knew firsthand how powerful he was in the water.

The sandy bottom appeared below. She swam a few more strokes then began to wade. The world spun as Constantine swung her into his arms, which was no easy feat. Apart from the fact that he had just swum a good distance, she was not small. She was five foot seven, and lean and toned because she regularly put in time at the pool, swimming laps. She also lifted weights and had progressed to the point where she could almost bench her own body weight, which, according to her gym instructor, was very cool. That all meant that she was a lot heavier than she looked.

She stiffened and tried to shimmy out of his grasp. And tried not to like that he was carrying her. In response, his arms tightened, holding her firmly against his chest.

Avoiding his interested gaze and the fact that he was barely out of breath, she shoved at his slick shoulders. "Okay, tough guy, you can let me go now."

Somewhere it registered that she had said at least some of those words before, the previous day. They hadn't done the trick then, either. She spied batteries and what looked like a camera memory stick scattered on her beach towel. There were some interesting scuffle marks in the sand. "What did you do with the reporter?"

"If you're looking for a shallow grave you won't find one. Although I admit I was tempted."

Constantine let her down on the sand. "Honey, I wasn't there when your father had the heart attack," he said quietly. "I didn't know he had a heart condition. He was at a casino instead of attending the meeting he had requested with me when he had the attack. One of my men, Tomas, got him out of there before the newspapers could get hold of the story. Unfortunately, someone leaked details. Probably the same person who went to the newspapers about the loan."

He had tried to protect them. For a moment Sienna's mind went utterly blank. She was so shocked by what he had done that his calling her "honey" barely registered.

She sucked in a deep breath, but the oxygen didn't seem to be getting through. It registered that the fast swim after an almost sleepless night had not been a smart move, her head felt heavy and pressurized, her knees wobbly. When her vision started to narrow and fade she knew she was going to faint for the first time in her life.

"This is not happening." Her hand shot out, automatically groping for support.

Constantine's arm was suddenly around her waist, holding her steady. The top of her head bumped his chin. The scrape of his stubbled jaw on the sensitive skin of her forehead sent a reflexive shiver through her, and suddenly she had her sight back. She inhaled. His warm male scent, laced with the clean, salty smell of the sea, filled her nostrils.

As if a switch had been thrown, she was swamped by memories, some hot and sensuous, some hurtful enough that her temper roared to life. She stiffened, lurching off balance despite the support.

Constantine said something curt beneath his breath. His arm tightened, an iron bar in the small of her back. When she next focused on him, she was sitting on the sand with Constantine holding her head down between her knees.

"I'm okay now," she told him.

The pressure on her neck disappeared. She lifted her head and blinked at the brilliance of sun and sand. Constantine was sitting beside her, his arms resting on his drawn-up knees. The moment seemed abruptly surreal. It suddenly occurred to her how different Constantine was at the beach, almost as if when he walked onto the sand he shed his responsibilities along with his clothes.

A vibrating sound caught her attention, a cell phone ringing. She looked around and spotted his clothes, an expensive suit, shirt and tie and designer shoes lying in an untidy pile on the sand. She made a covert study of Constantine. He wasn't wearing swimming trunks, just dark gray boxers, the wet fabric hugging the powerful muscles of his thighs.

Constantine made no move toward his phone.

"Aren't you going to answer that?"

His expression was surprisingly relaxed, almost con-nt. "No."

"Why not?"

His mouth kicked up at the corner. "I don't answer hones at the beach."

She found herself smiling back at him. In this, at least, ey were the same. She regularly "ran away" to the beach, eeding the uncomplicated casualness of sun and sand, the eeling of utter freedom the water gave her.

She hadn't ever applied those needs to Constantine, but e did now and a sharp tug of grief for everything they ad lost pulled at her. Since the breakup she had been so ocused on the things that had gone wrong, she hadn't anted to remember the wonderful moments.

She sifted sand between her fingers. "Then you should robably go to the beach more often."

His gaze rested on hers with an odd, neutral look. For e first time she acknowledged that when Constantine had alked away from her, his emotional cut-off hadn't been s clinical as she had imagined. He had lost, too.

With a final twitch the phone stopped vibrating.

"Why would you even consider helping my father?" nstead of avoiding his gaze, Sienna let herself be pinned y it. Not because she wanted the contact, but because she eeded to establish that Constantine was telling the truth out what had happened.

"I'm not a monster. I was willing to talk."

"You were there to collect." She didn't come right out nd say he had killed her father, but the thought loomed rge in her mind.

"Now that's where you're wrong." Constantine's aze was unnervingly direct. "Your father contacted

me and made the arrangement to meet. I wasn't ther
to collect. He wanted another loan."

A few minutes before eight, Sienna stepped into a
ankle-length, midnight blue silk shift and ruthlessl
squashed the heady sense of anticipation that had bee
building ever since those few minutes on the beach. Sh
had to keep reminding herself that Constantine was forc
ing her to meet him at a social event; this wasn't a date.

She checked her makeup, which she'd spent severa
minutes applying. Her hair was coiled in a classic kno
The Ambrosi pearls she was wearing were the only lavis
note. Part of a sample collection they were using to wo
a European retail giant, de Vries, the flowerlike cluster o
pearls at each lobe and the choker, made from a string o
pearl flowers, looked both modern and opulent.

She was attending Constantine's cocktail party at hi
command, but that didn't mean she couldn't use the oppor
tunity to promote her company. An Atraeus Group mee
and greet translated to a room filled with clients and sale
contacts Ambrosi Pearls desperately needed.

The car arrived just before eight.

Carla, who had hovered in her bedroom while Sienn
had dressed discussing the loan situation, followed he
downstairs. Carla was Ambrosi's PR guru, she was als
the current Face of Ambrosi, a cost-cutting move that ha
made sense because Carla was outrageously gorgeous an
photogenic.

Carla watched as Sienna checked that she had he
phone, credit card and house key. "I'll wait up for you. I
you need help, call me or text, and I'll come and get you

Sienna pinned a determined smile on her face. "Thank
but that won't be necessary. Believe me, this is strictl
business."

She braced for the next confrontation with Constantine as she stepped out into the courtyard. Instead, a lean, dark man who introduced himself as Tomas, Constantine's personal assistant, opened the passenger door of a sleek sedan.

Disappointment flattened her mood as Sienna climbed into the expensive, leather-scented interior. Despite the tension, after the interlude on the beach, she had been certain Constantine had been more than a little interested in picking up where they had previously left off. Evidently, she had been wrong. If Constantine had wanted to underline the power he held, he couldn't have done it more effectively than this.

Twenty minutes later, Tomas turned into a gated drive flanked by security and parked outside an impressive colonial mansion. Sienna took in the sleek, expensive cars that lined the gravel driveway and the lush, tropical garden lit by glowing lights as she mounted the steps to the front door. A brief security check later and she was shown into a chandelier-lit room.

She glimpsed Constantine, dark and brooding in a black suit and fitted black T-shirt, at one end of the crowded room. Jaw firming, she started toward him, her eyes narrowed assessingly as she studied the wealthy, influential crowd. Her heart sped up at the thought that there could even be a de Vries representative here and she would have the opportunity to apply a little direct pressure.

Her way was abruptly blocked by Alex Panopoulos, one of Ambrosi's most prestigious clients.

Panopoulos, the CEO of an Australasian retail empire, had tried to date both her and Carla on several occasions. Since Panopoulos had a reputation as a likeable rogue and a playboy, deflecting him socially hadn't been difficult. He took the rebuffs with good humor; the only problem was he kept bouncing back.

"Sienna." Panopoulos took both of her hands in his. "I was sorry to hear about your father. I was out of the country until this afternoon, otherwise I would have attended the funeral. Did you get my flowers?"

The "flowers" were an enormous arrangement of hothouse orchids that had cost a small fortune and which Carla had given to an elderly neighbor. "Yes, thank you." She flexed her fingers, wondering when he was going to release them. Simultaneously, she sent small darting glances around the room trying to spot the de Vries rep, Harold Northcliffe, a short, plump man who had a reputation for being elusive.

Panopoulos ignored the small movements. "And...how is the business?"

Sienna held on to her professional veneer with difficulty. "We closed today, but otherwise, it's business as usual."

He released one hand and brushed the delicate skin beneath one eye. "With your usual efficiency, no doubt. It's good to take care of business, but I think you also need to take care of yourself."

For a brief moment in time, Sienna almost wished she could have felt something for Panopoulos, even though she knew this was part of his routine, as practiced and slick as his formidable management skills.

Panopoulos smiled, signaling that he was closing in for the kill. "As a matter of fact, I'm very glad we've met tonight. I was hoping you might have dinner with me next week."

Sienna stiffened. Panopoulos was canny. She suspected that he deliberately kept in touch with both her and Carla on a personal level in order to gain an inside track on acquiring Ambrosi, should the business falter. "If you're worried about what the papers are printing, don't be. Ambrosi Pearls will continue to supply your orders."

The calculating glint in his eye grew stronger, more direct. "I'm sure that is so. But it was the future I wanted to discuss."

His grip on her remaining hand tightened. With a start, Sienna realized he meant to lift her fingers to his mouth.

"Panopoulos."

He dropped her fingers as if they had suddenly become red-hot. "Atraeus."

Constantine's gaze briefly locked with hers before he turned his attention back to Panopoulos. "I hear you're joining us on Medinos for the opening of our newest resort complex."

Panopoulos's expression was carefully blank. "I appreciate the opportunity to establish a retail outlet on Medinos. Seven-star hotels are thin on the ground."

"I understand you've made a substantial bid for floor space for the second stage of the resort complex?"

"I spoke with Lucas a few minutes ago. He's set up a preliminary meeting."

"In that case, I'll look forward to seeing you on Medinos next week. Now, if you'll excuse us, Ms. Ambrosi and I have a business matter to discuss."

Panopoulos's gaze narrowed at the smooth dismissal. "Of course."

Constantine's palm landed in the small of her back, burning through the silk and sending a shock of awareness through her as he urged her past Panopoulos.

Seconds later they stepped out of the crowded reception room and onto a deserted patio. Enclosed by walls and cascading foliage, the outdoor space was lushly tropical. A tinkling fountain added an exotic note, and gardenias released their perfume into air that was still sultry from the afternoon storms.

Annoyed by the high-handed way he had dispensed with Panopoulos then marched her away, Sienna stepped back from Constantine, deliberately using a patio chair to create even more space between them. "You shouldn't have done that. I was in discussion with a client. Alex is one of Ambrosi's best custom—"

"What did he want?"

The grim register of Constantine's voice intensified the distracting, humming awareness. The potent attraction made no sense; she should have been over it long ago. "That's none of your business."

"If Panopoulos wanted to discuss Ambrosi, then that is my business."

The soft reminder of just how much power Constantine wielded over her family's company, and her, strengthened the notion that he wasn't in the least unhappy with the situation. "Our discussion was personal. As it happened, he was asking me out to dinner."

"You turned him down."

His flat assertion that she had no interest in Alex contrarily made her bristle. "As a matter of fact, I didn't." Which wasn't a lie, because Constantine had intervened before she could turn him down.

He said something curt beneath his breath. "You're aware that it's Ambrosi Pearls that Panopoulos wants?"

Annoyance exploded inside her, the burst of temper a welcome change from the uncharacteristic jittery angst that had overtaken her since the conversation at her father's gravesite. "Yes. Now, if you'll excuse me—"

"Not yet."

The soft demand froze her in place. Light washed over the sharp cut of his cheekbones, highlighting the irritable glitter of his eyes. In that moment she registered that Constantine wasn't just angry, he was furious.

She had only ever seen him furious once before—the day they had broken up—but on that occasion he had been icily cool and detached. The fact that his formidable control had finally slipped and he was clearly in danger of losing his temper ratcheted the tension up several notches.

A heady sense of anticipation gripped her. She had the feeling that they were standing on some kind of emotional precipice, that for the first time she was going to see the real Constantine and not the controlled tycoon who had a calculator in place of a heart.

Overhead, thunder rumbled; the air was close and tropically hot. In the distance an electrical storm flickered.

Great. Just what she needed, to be reminded of the previous afternoon's encounter and her complete and utter loss of composure.

"Has he proposed?"

Sienna drew in a sharp breath. If she didn't know better, she could almost swear that Constantine was jealous. "Not yet."

"And if he does?"

"If he does…" She searched for something, anything, to say that would reduce her vulnerability. "I'll have to consider saying yes. It's a fact that this time, with a family and business to care for, when it comes to marriage, business does count. Right now, as far as I'm concerned a husband with money would be win-win."

"When Panopoulos finds out how much Ambrosi owes, he won't place your relationship on a formal footing."

Sienna's heart pounded out of control when he shifted the patio chair and glided closer, looming over her in the small courtyard, his breath stirring her hair.

His gaze dropped to her mouth and she was suddenly unbearably aware that he intended to kiss her.

Six

Sienna retreated a step. Big mistake. She had allowed herself to be cornered, literally. One more step and she would come up against the courtyard wall. "I find that remark offensive."

"It would only offend if you'd slept with Panopoulos, and I don't think you have."

Her jaw firmed. She had made a mistake, dangling Panopoulos in front of Constantine, but it was too late to backtrack now. "You can't be sure of that."

"I've been in town for four days. When I wasn't trying to contact you, I made some inquiries. It wasn't difficult to obtain information."

Her stomach sank. With his resources, Constantine would have found it ridiculously easy to discover whatever he wanted to know about her, including the fact that her personal life was as arid as a desert. She seldom dated. She didn't have time to date; she was too busy trying to sell pearls. "You've got no right to pry into my private affairs."

"It's not exactly what I had planned for my leisure time, either, but whether we like it or not, for the foreseeable future, everything to do with Ambrosi Pearls and you is my business. Have you discussed the loan with Brian Chin yet?"

The sudden change from personal to business threw her even more off balance. Brian Chin was Ambrosi's accountant. "I faxed the pages to him this afternoon. He wasn't happy."

An understatement. Like her, Brian had been in a state of shock.

"I take it Chin is still the extent of your financial advice?"

"Brian's been with us for ten years; he's loyal."

"But not a player. He could never control your father."

"Who could?" Even though she felt disloyal to her bluff, charismatic father, it was a relief to finally say the words.

Impatience registered in his gaze. "Then why did you try?"

"Someone had to. Mom doesn't have a head for business. Neither does Carla. If I hadn't stepped in we would have lost everything a long time ago."

"I would have helped."

Her jaw squared. "You had your chance."

His gaze narrowed at her reference to the financial deal that had ended their engagement. "Not under those conditions."

"If you'd bothered to find out anything about me at all, you would have known how important Ambrosi is to me."

"I knew. Why do you think I walked?"

Shock reverberated through her. In a moment of clarity,

she saw herself as she had been two years ago, just seconds ago—driven, obsessed.

The fact that Constantine had ended their engagement so quickly was no longer incomprehensible. She had always known he was ruthless and uncompromising in business; she just hadn't translated that reality to his personal life. He hadn't liked being left out of the picture and he hadn't been prepared to take second place to either her father's gambling addiction or Ambrosi Pearls.

"Finally, you get it."

And suddenly he was close, too close. An automatic step back and the chill of the masonry wall, a stark contrast to the potent heat of his body, brought her up short. Lightning flickered, the display increasingly spectacular, followed by a growl of thunder.

She should shimmy out, slip past him. A quick call to a taxi firm and five minutes on the roadside and she would be on her way home. If Constantine wanted a discussion it would have to be over the phone, or with lawyers present.

His hand landed on the wall beside her head, cutting off that avenue of escape. "Why didn't you tell me what was going on two years ago?"

"And watch you walk away, like you did when you found out about the proposed loan?"

"I told you, I would have helped."

For a moment her mind went utterly blank. Until then she hadn't realized how angry she had been at Constantine for walking away, for choosing not to even try to understand her predicament when she had desperately needed his support. "And then walked? Thanks, but no thanks."

"You could have used professional help for your father and the business."

"He wouldn't accept the first, and we couldn't afford the second."

The pad of his thumb slid along the line of her jaw. Her pulse pounded out of control, her body's response to the sudden stifling intimacy of his touch intense and unsettling.

She felt caught and held by emotions she didn't want to feel: anger, frustration and, unacceptably, a heady, dizzying anticipation. Ever since those loaded moments in his car, she realized she had been waiting for Constantine to make a move on her.

He muttered a short, rough Medinian phrase. "Why are you so stubborn?"

"I guess it's an Australian trait."

Reminding Constantine that after the Second World War, the Ambrosi family had chosen to uproot themselves from Medinos and make Australia their home was a tenuous counterpunch. But in that moment she was willing to grasp at anything that separated her from Constantine.

His hold was gentle enough that she could slide away, walk away if she wanted…

She saw the moment he logged her decision, the intent in his gaze as he angled her jaw so that her mouth was mere inches from his. She also learned something else. If she was still blindly, fatally attracted to Constantine, it was an unsettling fact that he also wanted her, and suddenly there was no air.

Constantine's mouth brushed hers. Sienna jerked back in an effort to control the heat that shimmered through her. She shouldn't want to know what touching him again—kissing him—would feel like when she had spent two years working doggedly to forget. "This isn't fair."

He grinned quick and hard. "It wasn't meant to be."

His hands settled at her waist. Now was the time to pull

back, to insist that they keep their relationship on a business footing.

Instead, seduced by the mesmerizing fact that he did still want her, that if she wasn't careful she could fall for him again, she lifted up on her toes, cupped his jaw and kissed him back.

A bolt of heat seared straight to her loins. She could feel his fingers in her hair, the sharp tug as he pulled out pins, the soft slide of her hair over her shoulders.

He cupped her breast through the double layer of silk and her bra. Her stomach clenched and for a timeless moment she hung suspended. Until a masculine voice registered and she was free, cool air circulating against her overheated skin.

Constantine controlled the savage desire to dismiss Tomas, who was hovering at the entrance to the courtyard.

His PA was under strict instructions not to interrupt this interlude, or let anyone else do so, which meant that whatever Tomas had to say was urgent.

Positioning himself so that he blocked Sienna from Tomas's view, and the curious stares they were now attracting from the handful of guests who had drifted near the French doors, Constantine took the phone Tomas handed him and answered the call.

The conversation with his chief financial advisor was brief and to the point. The legal tangle his father and Roberto Ambrosi had concocted between them had resulted in an unexpected hitch. Lorenzo had signed away water rights Constantine needed for Roberto's bogus pearl enterprise. No water rights meant no marina development, which effectively froze a project in which he had already invested millions.

Constantine terminated the call and handed the phone back to Tomas. Dismissing him with curt thanks, he turned back to Sienna. He had expected that in the brief interval it had taken to deal with the phone call she would close off from him, and he wasn't wrong. Grimly, he noted that in the space of less than two minutes she had smoothed her hair back into an elegant knot, found her evening bag, which she had dropped, and recovered the cool composure that irked him so much.

A jagged flash of lightning signaled that the violent electrical storm had rolled overhead. Sienna, he noticed, didn't so much as flinch. Her gaze was already focused on his room of retailers and, no doubt, the prospect of closing a number of lucrative sales deals.

Not for the first time it occurred to him that he might have more success with Sienna if he had one of her order sheets in his hand.

When she would have strolled past him, using the avenue of an interested group of spectators who had strolled out onto the courtyard to view the pyrotechnics as an escape route, Constantine blocked her way.

"We haven't finished our discussion." He indicated the softly lit decking that encircled the ground level of the house. "We can conclude our business in the privacy of my study."

Sienna teetered on the brink of refusing, the danger inherent in a private meeting suddenly vastly more potent than the financial threat.

In the end, though, she nodded and mounted the veranda steps, eager to at least get under cover. "I take it the phone call was bad news?"

Constantine's calmness was utterly at odds with the white-hot intensity of the kiss. "Nothing that can't be handled."

The call had been bad news, but that suited Sienna. A return to animosity would be a relief, neutralizing the panicked notion that Constantine was intent on maneuvering her back into his bed.

A hot pulse of adrenaline went through her as the thought gathered momentum. She should never have kissed him back. It had been a reckless experiment. She had practically thrown herself at him. Temporarily at least, it had altered the equation between them, giving him a power over her she had vowed he would never again have.

As if to underscore her imminent danger, a deafening clap of thunder sent her wobbling off balance. One stiletto jammed in a knot in the decking timber and in that moment the lights went out, plunging them into darkness.

Constantine's arm curved around her waist. She found herself pressed against the hard outline of his body, her breasts flattened against his chest. She registered the firm shape of his arousal pressed against her stomach. Heated awareness flashed. Reflexively, she shoved at his chest and bent down to release her foot from the stuck shoe. As she straightened, her head connected solidly with Constantine's jaw in a replay of what had happened the previous day.

Constantine lurched off balance. A second white-hot flash illuminated the fact that on this particular stretch of veranda there was no railing to halt his fall, just a sculpted patch of shrubbery. In the next instant they were plunged back into pitch-blackness.

Panic burned through Sienna as she pulled off her remaining shoe, tossed it on the deck along with her evening bag, and gingerly felt her way to the edge of the decking. Hitching her dress up, she climbed into the garden, picking her way through a collection of rocks and succulents, to find Constantine. Lightning flickered again, illuminating him as he pushed into a sitting position.

"Where am I?"

She grabbed his arm. "In the garden."

He rubbed at his jaw, making her feel instantly guilty. That was the second time she had hit him in the same spot.

"Figures."

Bracing her arm around his waist she helped him up, staggering under his weight.

Her dress was catching on the spiky leaves of some tropical flower. Something both crunchy and soft squished under her bare foot. Not a plant.

They stepped onto cool, damp grass. Constantine's arm tightened around her waist, tucking her firmly against his side, until they made their way to a line of solar garden lights that illuminated a path. Seconds later they climbed a shallow series of steps back onto the veranda.

From the controlled tautness of his muscles, the smooth way he moved, Sienna had a sudden suspicion that Constantine no longer needed her support, if he had ever needed it at all.

The click of a door latch punctuated the now distant rumble of thunder. Groping for reference points in the darkness, Sienna's fingers brushed over the smooth painted surface of a doorframe.

Another step and she was inside, her bare feet sinking into thick carpet. The door slammed, cutting off sound. The darkness was warmer and hushed here, scented with the springlike freshness of flowers and a rich undernote of leather. It did not smell like a working environment. "Where are we?"

"My private suite. The study is just down the hall."

Constantine leaned back against the door. Sienna's hand shot out, landing on the taut muscles of his abdomen. His arm tightened around her waist, sealing her against the seductive heat of his chest, and she was made shiveringly aware that Constantine was showing no inclination to move.

Resisting the counterproductive urge to stay put, Sienna disentangled herself and stepped free. She was now certain that, apart from his initial dazed state, there was nothing wrong with Constantine. She peered into the stygian darkness and injected a note of briskness into her voice. "Tell me where you keep a flashlight or candles."

"There's a flashlight in the bedroom."

She was not falling for that one. "In that case you can stay here. I'm going to get help."

And right after she found one of Constantine's minions, she would call for a taxi. He would have all the help he needed. There would be no need for her to come back and check on him.

His fingers locked with hers in the darkness, anchoring her in place. "I don't need help."

Lightning flashed through the leaded sidelights on either side of the door, illuminating the darkening bruise on Constantine's jaw.

She inhaled sharply. "I did hurt you."

"Tell me about it," he murmured and drew her toward him.

His mouth came down on hers, his lips warm and unexpectedly soft. Suddenly, leaving was not an option. Lifting up on her toes, she wound her arms around his neck and returned the kiss with interest. Any idea that Constantine was truly hurt or vulnerable dissolved. If he had been stunned by the fall, clearly the effects had worn off because he was fully aroused.

Long minutes later, he lifted her into his arms, negotiated the hall and carried her into a darkened room, his night vision unerring as he located a couch and set her down on it.

As she went to work on the buttons of his shirt, she felt the zipper of her dress release, then the fastening of her bra. Another long, searing kiss and Constantine peeled both garments away.

Lightning, paler and more distant now, flickered as he jerked his tie free and shrugged out of the jacket and the shirt. His weight came down on her, the bare skin of his chest hot against her breasts. For long breathtaking moments they continued to kiss with a drugging, seducing sweetness that spun her back to long afternoons in her apartment, even longer nights in his bed.

His fingers hooked in the waistband of her panties. She lifted her hips and with one gliding movement she was naked aside from the pearls in her lobes and at her throat.

She had a brief moment to consider that she was on the verge of making a monumental mistake before deciding that after the past two years of worry and work, she could do what she wanted just this once. She could give in to the exhilarating passion she had thought had died when Constantine had walked out on her.

The feel of his trousers against her inner thighs as he came down between her legs was a faint irritation, signaling that Constantine wasn't naked. She had thought, in the brief interval that he had separated himself from her that he would have dispensed with his pants altogether. That small detail faded into insignificance as finally, achingly, they came together.

Until that moment she hadn't realized how much she had missed him, missed this. She had loved the touch, the taste, the feel of him, loved the intimacy of making love, the way he'd made her feel when they'd been together.

Constantine murmured something rough in Medinian. "I knew it. You haven't been with anyone else."

Sienna was momentarily distracted by the satisfaction

in his voice, then his mouth closed over one breast and hot pleasure zapped conscious thought, and she could only clasp his shoulders and move with him.

She heard his indrawn breath. The pressure was close to unbearable, holding her on a knife's edge of expectation, and in a moment of shock she realized he was wearing a condom. She hadn't been aware that he had put one on. Aside from the occasional distant flicker of lightning outside it was pitch-black, and for long, dizzying minutes she'd been blindly absorbed by the overwhelming sensations.

The brief span of time when she had thought he had been undressing was now explained. He had been performing a much more important task.

She should be grateful that he hadn't lost his head the way she had, that he had protected them both, but the knowledge that he had condoms with him was abruptly depressing. A man didn't carry condoms unless he expected, or planned, to make love.

He began to move and her breath hitched in her throat. With every gliding stroke the pleasure wound tighter and tighter. She coiled her arms around his neck, burying her face against his shoulder as the burning tension gathered. Her climax finally hit her in shimmering, incandescent waves. Dimly she was aware of Constantine's release just seconds after her own, the moment primal and extreme.

Soft golden light flooded the room with shocking suddenness. Constantine's gaze locked with hers and any doubt that the lovemaking had been a spur of the moment decision on his part evaporated when she saw the possessive satisfaction in his eyes. However random the events that had precipitated this interlude appeared, he *had* planned to make love to her.

She stirred beneath Constantine's weight, with an effort

of will controlling the intense emotions that had temporarily hijacked her brain, and the hurt. She had wanted to believe that Constantine had been as swept away as she had been.

She pushed at his shoulders. Obligingly, he shifted to one side, allowing her to scramble off the couch.

Feeling exposed and more than a little flustered, she found her dress. Stepping into it, she quickly fastened the zipper. Her bra was hooked over one end of the couch, and she spied her panties beneath an elegant coffee table.

Constantine was in the process of fastening his pants. Cheeks burning, she averted her gaze from his sleek, bronzed shoulders and lean hips. Instead, she snatched up the panties and made a beeline for the bathroom.

Feeling increasingly horrified at her lack of control, she stared at her reflection in the large mirror positioned over a marble vanity. Her hair was disheveled, her skin flushed, her mouth swollen. Constantine might have planned to make love to her, but that didn't change the fact that she had practically thrown herself at him—not once, but twice. And he had been quite happy to take advantage of her vulnerability.

A few minutes later, freshened up, her hair finger combed, she ventured back out into the sitting room. The dress had smoothed out against the warmth of her skin, but she was still minus her shoes and her clutch, which were both outside on the veranda.

Constantine was pacing the room talking into a cell phone, his expression taut. He had pulled on a fresh shirt, which he had left unbuttoned. Her gaze skittered away from the mouthwatering slice of tanned chest and washboard abs. The sexy casualness of his attire emphasized the intimacy of what they had just shared.

Constantine terminated the call and slipped the phone into his pocket.

"Problems?" Suddenly in a hurry to leave, she circled the room, giving the large leather sofa a wide berth as she inched toward the door.

Constantine's silvery gaze tracked her. "A hitch with the new resort."

"Which is why you're flying out tonight."

There was an oddly weighted pause. "You could come with me."

For a brief second, despite the hurt and disillusionment, dizzying temptation pulled at her. "To Medinos?"

He glanced at his watch. "I fly out in three hours. You're welcome to share the flight with me. It makes sense," he concluded smoothly. "We haven't had time to...complete our business. We can pick up where we left off."

In his bed.

Sienna squashed the wild impulse to say yes, to immerse herself even more deeply in a relationship that logic and history dictated was destined to crash and burn.

The sensible response was to refuse, to put their relationship back on a business footing.

Her fingers automatically went to the pearl choker at her throat. She forced herself to breathe, to think. This was no longer just about her.

An Atraeus Resort opening was an A-list event, by invitation only. It would be jam-packed with high-end press and industry professionals. All of the luxury retail giants would be represented, including de Vries.

Despite what had happened on the couch, going to Medinos was an opportunity she couldn't afford to pass up.

She would never have a better chance to push Ambrosi Pearls' new range and secure the sales contract they had been chasing. If de Vries signed even a one-year deal, they could pay off Constantine. They would be free and clear. "All right."

Surprise flared in Constantine's gaze and was just as quickly controlled. "Tomas will take you home so you can pack your bag."

She thought quickly. Apart from the fact that she didn't want to be closeted alone with Constantine on a luxury corporate jet, this was a business trip; she needed time to prepare. Namely to pick up the samples from the vault at the office and make an appointment to meet with the de Vries representative attending the opening. The process of arranging the meeting was a delicate business, which could take days. "I can't go to Medinos tonight. I'll need two days before I leave."

Constantine's gaze narrowed at the sudden crispness of Sienna's voice, at odds with her softly flushed cheeks and tousled hair. His mood deteriorated further as she fingered the silky pearls at her throat for the third time and counting.

When they had been making love, the pearls had seemed to glow in the dark, reminding him that he wasn't just making love to the woman he wanted, he was making love to the CEO of Ambrosi Pearls.

Now she was backing off fast—from the lovemaking and from the unspoken admission he had forced from her that, deny it as she might, she still wanted him.

But at least she had agreed to come to his country, which was progress.

The idea had crystallized when she had stated that she would consider marriage with Panopoulos, then it had set in stone when he had discovered that she hadn't slept with anyone in the two years since their break up.

The primitive surge that had gripped him when he had

realized that Sienna, who had been a virgin when they had first made love, had never belonged to anyone but him, had been profound.

The thought that she could take another lover, possibly Panopoulos, made him break out in a cold sweat. That scenario was unacceptable. "In that case, let me know a departure time and I'll make the company jet available to you."

"No." Her chin jerked up, dark eyes shooting fire at the concept of him paying for her travel, underlining the fact that she was backing off, fast. "I'll book a commercial flight."

In a room filled with soft gold light and pooling shadows, suddenly the Medinian part of her ancestry, the long line of alchemists and merchants stretching back into antiquity, was starkly evident. His jaw tightened as the fascination that had gripped him the first time he had seen her struck him anew. "You can't afford the commercial flight."

By his calculations, he had been paying for everything, including her salary for the past two months.

Her cheeks flushed a deeper shade of pink. "I have money of my own."

"Then at least let me organize your ride home." He took out his phone and dialed Tomas before she could argue.

Seconds later he hung up and followed her out onto the veranda. Sienna had found her clutch and shoes.

Constantine crouched down and gently levered the stiletto heel out of a knot in the decking timber.

She took it from him, her movements brisk. As she slipped her foot into the shoe, she gripped the frame of a nearby window for balance. He caught her studying his reflection in the glass and satisfaction curled through him.

If Sienna had been indifferent to him, he would have

expedited the paperwork, which was cut-and-dried, and walked away. But she did want him. Their chemistry was hot enough to burn.

The fact that he was jealous of Panopoulos didn't please him. The uncomfortable reality that he still wanted Sienna after she had broken his trust two years ago was even more difficult to accept.

There was nothing logical about the emotions. He didn't want the attraction, but it existed, the pull absolute and powerful.

Tomas appeared, a set of keys in one hand. Sienna shot Constantine a bright, professional smile, her gaze missing his by inches as she hurried after Tomas.

As if she couldn't wait to be gone.

Gingerly, Constantine probed at the lump that had formed on the back of his head, clearly from one of his expensive and strategically placed landscape rocks.

He studied the now floodlit grounds and the patch of crushed bromelia balansae.

Damn. He couldn't believe he had fallen into the garden.

Seven

Two days later Sienna disembarked from her commercial flight into the searing heat of Medinos. The ice-blue cotton shift she was wearing was already sticking to her skin as she strolled into the arrivals terminal and found Tomas waiting for her.

Her stomach tensed against a twinge of what was, unacceptably, disappointment. During the flight she had been too wound to sleep, anticipating seeing Constantine when she landed.

Minutes later, with her luggage loaded into the trunk, Sienna slid dark glasses onto the bridge of her nose and settled into the passenger seat of a sleek, modern sedan. While Tomas drove, she stared curiously at limestone villas, fields of olives and grapes and an endless vista of sea and sky.

She had expected Medinos, with its wild, hard country, to be fascinating and she wasn't disappointed. Constantine and his family now owned vast tracts, some in plantations and farms. The original goat farm and market garden on the island of Ambrus was now, of course, a fabulously wealthy gold mine. In fact, the entire island of Ambrus was now owned by the Atraeus family.

From her research on the internet she'd discovered that the main island was large and well populated, although, because the interior was so rugged settlement was primarily on the coast. Other islands of the group were visible as they wound along a high precipitous road, appearing to float hazily in the distance. The lyrical names were as imbued with mystery and magic as the shimmering images: Nycea, Thais, Pythea and, closer in, Ambrus.

Tomas's cell phone rang, the buzz discreet. The low timbre of his voice as he spoke in rapid Medinian briefly spun her back to the explosive interlude with Constantine at his home.

When Sienna had exited the taxi that night after refusing to be driven by Tomas, Carla had been waiting.

Predictably, she had been horrified when she'd learned Sienna had decided to go to Medinos. "Please tell me you're not going with him."

"Don't worry." Sienna kept her voice crisp and light as she struggled to control her blush. "I'm traveling separately. This is business."

Although, very little of what they had done that night had even the remotest connection to business.

Dropping her evening bag on the kitchen table, she filled the electric jug with water and set it to boil. What she wanted was a steadying dose of caffeine but, since she needed to sleep, it was going to have to be herbal tea. As she turned to lean on the table, her reflection in the kitchen window flashed back at her. Tousled hair and bare mouth, the rich luster of pearls making her look more like a courtesan than the CEO of a company.

She had let him make love to her.

Guilty heat burned through her again at the instant, vivid recall of Constantine's mouth on hers, his muscular body pressing her into the soft leather couch.

Carla's expression was taut as she leaned against the frame of the kitchen door, her feet bare, her arms wrapping her thin silk robe closely around her waist. "I knew it. He wants you again."

"No." A little desperately, Sienna searched out painkillers, drank two down with a glass of water, then found mugs and tea bags, glad for the excuse to avoid Carla's too-sharp gaze. "At least, no more or less than he wants any woman."

"So, why does he want you to go to Medinos?"

She set the mugs on the table and dropped in the tea bags. "Not because he wants a relationship."

She poured hot water over the fragrant chamomile. What had happened on the couch had nothing to do with a relationship. It had been sex, pure and simple. Planned sex. Constantine had made no bones about wanting her and she hadn't been able to resist him.

Sienna removed the tea bags and handed Carla her mug. "I'm going to Medinos because a de Vries rep will be at the opening of the new Atraeus Resort. With any luck I can stall Constantine long enough to give us a chance to secure that contract."

A glimmer of hope entered Carla's eyes. She knew as well as Sienna that if they signed with de Vries they would be able to pay off the Atraeus loan outright. They would not lose Ambrosi Pearls.

"Hallelujah," Carla murmured. "Finally some light at the end of the tunnel. I just wish you didn't have to go to

Medinos. I don't trust the Atraeus men, and especially not Constantine. He doesn't have a reputation for revisiting anything—not mistakes, and definitely not affairs. Promise me that whatever you do, you won't let him make you his mistress. Nothing's worth that. Nothing."

Stung by the knowledge that even Carla now labeled her brief engagement to Constantine as an affair, Sienna sipped her tea. "The only liaison Constantine and I will be discussing is a business one."

Carla's cheeks were flushed, her jaw set. "Good. That's what I needed to hear. Be careful."

Sienna intended to be.

She turned her attention back to the glittering Medinian sea and a fishing boat maneuvering alongside a long narrow jetty. They were driving through the outskirts of a city now and the streets were increasingly busy. Olive-skinned, dark-eyed Medinians and brightly garbed tourists mingled, enjoying the brilliant sunshine and the vibrant market-style shopping and street cafés.

Tomas pointed out *Castello* Atraeus, a fortress built on the highest point of the headland, which overlooked the city of Medinos and the bay. Constructed of the same stone that many of the villas and cottages were made of, Sienna knew the original ancient *castello* which had once belonged to a noble family that had since died out, had been almost completely destroyed during the war. Lorenzo Atraeus had bought the ruin with his newfound wealth and had painstakingly rebuilt it, following the ancient designs.

Tomas briefly pointed out other buildings of significance including a magnificent modern library, which Lorenzo had gifted to the city, before driving along a curving stretch of beach. Minutes later, he turned into the lushly planted parking bay of The Atraeus Group's newest hotel—a sleek, luxury, seven-star resort that had only recently been completed.

As Sienna exited the car, her gaze was caught by the island that floated closest to Medinos. "Is that Ambrus?"

Tomas waited for the bellhop to load her bags. "Yes. That is Ambrus."

Looping the strap of her handbag over her shoulder, she walked into the air-conditioned paradise of the hotel's signature cream-and-gold foyer, with its intricately carved frescoes and exquisite mosaics.

Her heart thumped once, hard, when she glimpsed a head of coal-black hair brushing a familiar set of broad shoulders. Constantine was dressed casually in dark pants, a black T-shirt and a loose jacket. In the lush surroundings, he seemed even more darkly masculine and exotic than she remembered. His gaze locked with hers and any idea that this was a chance meeting evaporated.

Feeling overheated and a little flustered because she hadn't expected to encounter Constantine at the front desk, Sienna busied herself signing the register and collecting her key. Constantine spoke briefly with Tomas, directed the bellhop to her suite then insisted on accompanying her.

The lavish ground-floor suite he directed her to had both internal and external access, with huge glass sliding doors that framed an achingly beautiful view of Ambrus. Constantine unlocked the doors to a private patio.

Shielding her eyes against the sun, Sienna stepped outside and stared across the limpid blue water at towering black cliffs. High, rugged hills were bleached the color of ripe wheat by the sun, and the lower slopes were dotted by flashes of white, which she assumed were goats.

She had expected to feel a connection to Medinos. For years, just the name itself had entranced her, although the villa and pearl facility her family used to own were definitely past history.

Sienna logged the moment Constantine moved to stand beside her, her stomach clenching at the faint scents of aftershave and clean male. "Ambrus looks deserted."

Her gaze connected with his. For a split second she was spun back to the interlude at his house, the moment of clarity when the lights had come on and she had seen the possession in his eyes.

He indicated the island. "The mining company operates on the eastern side. There's a construction project for a new resort complex and marina on the northern headland. Other than that, we run goats to keep the weeds down. Your family's old pearl facility is based on the northwestern side."

She stared at the high, stark cliffs, the utter absence of anything as soft and tamed as a sandy beach. She knew there were calm bays and inlets—there had to be for the pearl beds—but there was nothing remotely civilized about the southern end.

A discreet tap on her door relieved her of her tingling awareness of Constantine and the hot flashes of memory that kept surfacing. Glad for an excuse to end the unnerving tension, Sienna walked through the elegant sitting room and opened the door so the bellhop could carry her bags inside.

Relieved to see her padlocked sample case stacked on top of her luggage, she tipped the lean young man. The future of Ambrosi Pearls was literally tied up in the contents of that case.

She started guiltily as Constantine prowled up behind her.

His gaze rested broodingly on the sample case, although he couldn't possibly know its contents.

He handed her two cream-colored embossed cards. The first was an invitation to the official opening of the resort that evening, the second an invitation to a luncheon to celebrate the product launch of a new collection of Atraeus gold jewelry the following day. "We won't have time to talk about the loan details today. That discussion will have to wait until this evening."

On the back of both cards, precisely handwritten—no doubt by Tomas or another of Constantine's people—were instructions on dress, reminding her that while Medinos might be a tourist destination, it was closer to the east in its moral codes than the west.

Cheeks flushed, she slipped the cards in her handbag, which was still looped over her shoulder. "Thank you."

Constantine stepped past her and paused at the open door. "I was certain you would appreciate the opportunity to circulate."

Sienna closed the door behind him and leaned against the cool wood waiting for the pounding in her chest to subside.

Constantine had seemed manageable in Sydney—barely. A mere hour ago she had been happily operating under the assumption that on a business footing, at least, she could handle him.

But this was not the Constantine she had known two years ago. The way he had seduced her so easily the other night was a case in point. He had ruthlessly used his fall and the power outage to maneuver her into having sex with him. The fact that she had wanted the sex wasn't at issue as much as the fact that Constantine was harder, sharper, more manipulative and dominant than she had bargained on.

And she was almost certain he knew exactly what she was up to on Medinos.

Eight

Constantine tracked Sienna's leisurely progress across the crowded reception room. Even if he hadn't been informed that she had entered the ballroom of Medinos's newest and most spectacular hotel, it would have been easy to spot her by the turning of heads as she strolled past.

Terminating a conversation, he placed his drink on a sideboard, his temper flashing to a slow burn when he saw what she was wearing.

Her hair was caught up in a knot, emphasizing the dress, which was designed to induce a stroke. A pale champagne halter, the gown was deceptively plain, the silky fabric an almost perfect match for the color of Sienna's skin so that at first glance he had thought she was naked. Added to that, the halter neck meant she wasn't wearing a bra.

His jaw tightened against a throb of mingled desire and irritation. Ankle length and discreetly cut, the gown paid lip service to the dress code he had demanded she follow, while subtly undermining it at every turn.

Beside him Lucas let out a low whistle.

"Look too long," Constantine said calmly, "and I'll put your eyes out."

When he had been dating Sienna, to avoid the press they hadn't gone out together at night. Normally, when he had been in Sydney, he had picked her up from work and taken her back to his apartment, or he'd followed her home to her place. The clothes she'd worn had been elegant, sleek, businesslike and sexy; he had barely noticed them.

The only other clothes he had seen had been her casual at-home gear, a bikini that had driven him crazy and her underwear, which for the most part had been tantalizing, but practical. What Sienna did or didn't have in her wardrobe hadn't interested him. Until now.

Zane, who had flown in from the States that morning for the resort opening, watched Sienna with his usual cool assessment. If Lucas was a shade on the wild side, Zane was worse, but he had the good sense to stay quiet about it. A couple of years on the streets of L.A. after he had run away from his mother's fourth marriage, and before they had managed to track him down, had left their mark. On the surface Zane was cool and calm with a killer charm. He never lacked for feminine company, but it was a fact that he didn't trust any of the women he had dated.

Zane sipped the beer he'd been nursing for the past twenty minutes. "It could be worth it. I notice she didn't bring her accountant with her."

Or anyone else, Constantine thought with grim satisfaction.

Lucas lifted a brow. "No briefcase, either."

No briefcase. No bra.

Zane took another swallow of his beer. "She doesn't look happy to be here."

Rub salt into the wound, Constantine thought bleakly. But at least she wasn't carrying that damned sample case.

"You don't need this," Lucas said bluntly.

Constantine's expression remained impassive. He hadn't discussed what had happened in Sydney, nor would he, but he was aware that Lucas knew exactly how focused he was on the CEO of Ambrosi Pearls.

He could have left the talking to their legal team. The options were clear-cut and his people were very, very good. Unless Sienna produced a large check, The Atraeus Group owned Ambrosi. But since those intense moments across the gravesite, this had ceased to be about the money.

At least for him.

He watched as Sienna paused to talk to an exquisitely dressed Japanese couple, her cool poise at odds with the off-the-register passion and fire that had seared him in Sydney.

The reason Sienna was in Medinos was simple. Aside from the fact that he wanted to make love to her again, he needed to know just how far she would go to clear the debt. The thought that she would agree to sleep with him in order to influence the negotiations wasn't something he wanted to dwell on, but after the debacle two years ago, and the fact that she had let him make love to her so easily the other night, he couldn't afford to ignore the possibility.

"The situation with the water rights has…complicated things," he explained to his brother.

Lucas shook his head. "The only real complication I can see is ten meters away and closing."

Zane finished his beer and set the glass down, his expression wry. "Ciao. Watch your back."

Constantine's gaze narrowed as a male guest moved

in on Sienna. His jaw tightened when he recognized Alex Panopoulos.

His phone vibrated. He registered the Sydney number of the security firm he had used to investigate the Ambrosi family. As he lifted the phone to his ear, Sienna turned to speak to Panopoulos. If he'd thought the front view of the dress was daring, the back of the gown was nonexistent. "It's not my back that's the problem."

Sienna managed to extricate herself from Alex Panopoulos on the pretext that she had to check her wrap. Pausing in a quiet alcove decorated with marble statuary and lush, potted palms, she folded the transparent length of champagne gauze into almost nothing and stuffed it into her evening bag. What she really wanted was a few moments to study the room and see if she could spot Northcliffe, the de Vries rep she was scheduled to meet with in the morning.

She caught a glimpse of Constantine, darkly handsome in evening dress as he talked into a cell phone, and her heart pounded hard.

Nerves still humming, she merged with the flow of guests while she examined that moment of raw panic.

Every time she remembered that she had encouraged Constantine to make love to her, her stomach clenched. Like it or not, where Constantine was concerned she was vulnerable, and the emotional risk of getting too close was high.

A waiter cruised past. She refused an array of canapés, too on edge to either eat or drink until she had identified Northcliffe. Pausing beside a glass display, she studied a series of gorgeously detailed pieces of jewelry, advance samples of tomorrow's product launch. For a timeless moment the room and the nervy anticipation dissolved and she was drawn into the fascinating juxtaposition of lucent tourmaline and smoothly worked gold.

She wasn't a designer. When it came to creating art or beautiful jewelry, she was utterly clueless. Her passion had always been the business side of things. Her father used to jokingly proclaim that she had the heart of a shopkeeper. It was a fact that she was never happier than when she was making a sale.

A faint tingling at her nape made her stiffen.

A glimpse of broad shoulders increased her tension.

If that was Constantine, then he had crossed the room, which meant he had seen her.

"Sienna. Glad you could make it."

She saw taut cheekbones and a tough jaw, but it wasn't Constantine. It was his younger brother, Lucas.

With his slightly battered features, courtesy of two seasons of professional rugby in Australia, and his smoldering bad-boy looks, he was undoubtedly hot.

Lucas had once tried to date Carla. Fatally, he had made his move after Constantine had walked out on Sienna and before Lucas had realized the wedding was off. Carla, who was loyal to a fault, had taken no prisoners and the public spat at a fabulous new nightclub had become the stuff of legend.

Magazines had lined up for the short time both Ambrosi girls had hit the publicity limelight, although Carla had handled the attention a lot better than Sienna. With her PR mind-set she had decided to view the fight with Lucas as a gold-plated opportunity to boost Ambrosi Pearls' profile, and thanks to her, orders had flooded in.

"You know me, Lucas." She checked out the last place she had seen Constantine. "Gold, jewels, objets d'art. I couldn't resist."

"You look like one of Constantine's objets d'art yourself."

Sienna countered his comment with a direct look. The dress she wore was sexier and more revealing than anything she would normally have worn to a business occasion, but in this case it was warranted. The gown had been used in their latest advertising campaign. Harold Northcliffe, who should have received the glossy press kit she had expressed to his Sydney office, would instantly recognize it. The jewelry itself was a set of prototypes they had designed with de Vries and the sophisticated European market in mind. "If you want to score points off me, Lucas, you're going to have to try harder than that. The dress belongs to Carla."

The amusement flashed out of his dark gaze. "It was the jewelry that really caught my eye."

"I didn't know you were interested in jewelry design." Lucas was known as The Atraeus Group's "hatchet man." His reputation was based more on corporate raiding than the creative arts.

"Not normally," he murmured, an odd note in his voice, "but I'm certain Constantine will be. When I first saw you I thought you were wearing a traditional set of Medinian bridal jewels. Quite a publicity stunt considering that you used to be engaged to Constantine."

Dismayed, Sienna touched the pearls at her throat. The pieces she was wearing were based on her grandfather Sebastien's original drawings. The delicate choker consisted of seed pearls woven into classical Medinian motifs, with a deep blue teardrop sapphire suspended from the center. Matching earrings with tiny drop sapphires dangled from her ears, and an intricate pearl bracelet studded with sapphires encircled her wrist.

"Speaking of the devil," Lucas murmured, looking directly over her shoulder.

A hot tingle ran down Sienna's spine. The knowledge that Constantine was directly behind her and closing in was so intense that for a moment she couldn't breathe.

Even though she was prepared, the confrontation was a shock. Dressed in a formal black evening suit, Constantine seemed taller, physically broader and, in that first moment, coldly remote. Although the impression of remoteness disappeared the instant she met his glittering gaze.

"We need to talk."

The curt demand sent another hot tingle through her. She resisted the urge to cross her arms over her chest. Suddenly the dress seemed too thin, too revealing, definitely not her best idea. "That is why I'm here."

A muscle pulsed along the side of his jaw. If she hadn't known he was angry before, she knew it then.

"Outside. Now."

Her jaw tightened at the low register of his voice, the unmistakable whiplash of command. "I don't think so." The last time she had taken orders she had been five and she had *wanted* that Barbie doll.

His hand closed around her arm; his palm burned into her naked skin. A pang of pure feminine fear shot through her, making all the fine hairs at her nape stand on end, but she dug her heels in. To anyone watching they would no doubt appear to be engaged in an intimately close conversation, but Constantine's grip was firm.

When her resistance registered, he bent close. His lips almost brushed her ear and his warm breath fanned her neck, sending another fiery pang through her, this time straight to her loins. She froze, pinned in place by the potent lash of sensation. For a split second she couldn't move. Worse, she didn't want to.

"We're leaving now. If you make a fuss, I'll carry you out and no one will stop me."

"You can't do this."

"Try me."

Wildly she checked for Lucas, but he had conveniently disappeared. "This is assault."

He laughed, and the weird primitive female thing that had frozen her in place and which was probably designed as a survival mechanism for the race so that women would have sex with men even if they were hideous and had no manners at all, dissolved. Suddenly, she was back. "I'll call the police."

"Before or after our business meeting tomorrow?"

Her teeth snapped together at his blatant use of the power he had over both her and Ambrosi. "That's blackmail."

He applied pressure, unceremoniously shunting her out of the room. "Babe, that's business."

Nine

Sienna dug in her high-heels as they entered a deserted gallery with tall, arched windows along one wall, softly lit works of art on the other. "This is as far as I go. We're out of the ballroom, which strangely enough you wanted to leave despite the fact that it's your party. But if we go any farther, I'm afraid no one will hear my screams."

"Calm down, I'm not interested in hurting you."

Ignoring her protest, Constantine swung her up into his arms.

Sienna pushed at his shoulders and attempted to wriggle free. "You could have fooled me."

Constantine strode a short distance then set her down directly in front of a large oil painting, grunting softly when her elbow accidentally caught him in the stomach.

Just when she was congratulating herself on finally ruffling his steely control, one long tanned finger flicked the sapphire teardrop just above the swell of her cleavage. "Part of the new promotion?"

Her cheeks burned with a combination of irked fury and a dizzying heat. "How would you know about that?"

"I'm still on your client mailing list. I get all of your pamphlets."

"I'll have to speak to my assistant."

Better still, she would edit the list herself. Those glossy pamphlets were too expensive to mail out to people who were never going to buy their products.

Constantine's expression was grim. "When you walked into the ballroom wearing Medinian bridal jewels you caused quite a stir. Was that planned, or a coincidence?"

She followed the direction of his gaze. The jewel-bright colors of the large oil painting that loomed overhead came into sharp focus. She studied what was, without doubt, a wedding portrait. "I had no idea these were wedding jewels."

"Or that the press could put two and two together and make ten." Constantine's expression was frustratingly remote. "This isn't a game, Sienna."

She flushed. The only thing she was guilty of was trying to save her family business and she would not apologize for that. "I'm not playing a game or pulling a publicity stunt."

Constantine folded his arms over his chest. "Prove it."

She was tempted to explain nothing, pack her bag and leave on the earliest flight out, but until the loan situation was resolved, she was stuck. "Very well. Come to my room and I'll show you."

Unlocking the door to her suite, she stepped inside and flicked a switch. Lights glowed softly over the marble floors and luxurious white-on-white furnishings.

She set her evening bag on a coffee table flanked by cream leather couches and walked to the wall safe. Punching in her PIN, she dragged out the sample case, which was sitting on top, removed her laptop then quickly shoved the sample case back in the safe, out of sight.

She placed the laptop, a girly pink model with all the latest bells and whistles, on the coffee table. Booting it up, she accessed the jewelry design files, which contained a photographed portfolio of designs that had belonged to her grandfather. She found the scanned page she wanted then removed the jewelry she was wearing and arranged it alongside the laptop. "These jewels are prototypes. They're not in production—"

"Until you locate a buyer."

Sienna drew a calming breath. "—until we have received expressions of interest."

"Otherwise known as a sales order."

Her jaw tightened. "The Ambrosi versions aren't an exact match of the jewels my grandfather sketched. The designs have merely been based on his drawings. We had no idea they were bridal jewelry."

Constantine was oddly still, the pooling lamplight softening the taut line of his jaw, the chiseled cheekbones and the faint hollows beneath. In the lamplight, with his coal-dark hair flowing to his shoulders, he looked fierce and utterly male, much as she had imagined ancient Medinian warriors must have looked. "It seems I owe you an apology."

"Not at all." Grimly, she powered the laptop down and then had to go through the whole risky rigmarole of taking the sample case back out of the safe in order to slot in the laptop.

"Allow me," Constantine said, smoothly taking the sample case from her grasp.

Heart pounding, Sienna reclaimed the case and jammed it back in the safe. If Constantine discovered she was here trying to make a deal with de Vries, that would not be good. With any luck, he hadn't seen the discreet branding on the case because the printed side had been facing away from him when he had taken it from her.

A tiny clinking sound drew her attention. Constantine had picked the necklace up off the coffee table. The delicate combination of pearls and sapphires looked even more fragile against his hands. He gently touched a pearl. Sienna shivered, as if his finger had stroked across her skin.

His gaze connected with hers. "So, who did you wear those pearls for, if it wasn't me?"

"I don't know what you mean." Desperate for a distraction, Sienna walked through to the small adjacent kitchenette and bar, opened a cupboard and found glasses.

After filling the glasses with chilled water from the fridge, she handed one to Constantine, taking care to avoid brushing his fingers.

Constantine finished his drink in two long swallows.

Intensely aware of his gaze on her, she placed her drink on the coffee table and gathered up the sample jewels. The sooner they were out of sight the happier she would feel. If she had understood the potential for disaster inherent in the Medinian designs, she would have stuck to the more modern flower-patterned pearls.

Walking through to her bedroom, she wrapped the jewels in a silk scarf and placed them in the top dresser drawer. She would put them back in the sample case and lock them in the safe once Constantine had left.

When she returned to the sitting room Constantine was pacing. He picked up a small bronze statuette then set it down almost immediately. If she didn't know better, she would think he was nervous.

He glanced at his watch. "Have you eaten?"

The complete change in tack startled her enough that she answered without thinking. "Not since the flight."

"Then I'll order dinner in." He picked up the sleekly modern phone, which was situated on an escritoire.

His suggestion was subtly shocking. Her heart sped up at the thought of spending any more time secluded and alone with Constantine. "No. I'm not hungry."

"You need to eat, and I've made you miss dinner. If you don't want to eat here, we can go somewhere more public."

Sienna considered her options. Constantine had made no bones about the fact that he wanted her. The realization that she was actually contemplating sleeping with him again stopped her in her tracks.

Just days ago she hadn't been ready for a sexual relationship with anyone. Yet, despite being burned twice by Constantine, a stubborn part of her was still dizzily, irresistibly attracted.

Sex had to be out of the question.

She was here on business. For her family and Ambrosi Pearls' sake she had to stay focused.

To shield her blush, she busied herself with the unnecessary job of checking the lock on the safe. "I do need to eat, but not here."

If they ate out it would be easier to avoid talking business and it was a fact that she needed to stall Constantine until late morning at least. By then she would know whether or not de Vries was going to place an order.

"Suits me."

Constantine's unexpectedly mild tone was surprising. For a moment, she thought she saw relief in his gaze, which didn't make sense.

Confused, she walked to her bedroom and grabbed a silk shrug that would cover her bare shoulders and décol-

letage better than the wrap she'd worn earlier. When she
returned to the sitting room, Constantine was replacing
the telephone receiver.

"I've booked a table at a small café on the waterfront."

"Sounds great." She sent him her brightest, most professional smile. At this time of year, the height of the tourist
season, a waterfront café would be crowded. They would
be lucky to hear themselves think, let alone talk. A business discussion would be out of the question.

She picked up her evening bag and her key, and pre-
ceded Constantine through the door. She glimpsed their
reflection in the ornate hall mirror as they strolled out
of the suite. Constantine was tall, broad-shouldered and
remote in his formal evening dress. She looked unexpectedly provocative, the soft silk clinging to her curves as she
walked.

A powerful sense of déjà vu gripped her as she closed
the door behind her, laced with a cocktail of emotions she
thought she had dealt with, and dismissed, two years ago.

The image could have been a film clip from the past.
They had looked like a couple. They had looked like
lovers.

Renewed panic gripped her when she considered that
technically they were lovers. That all she had to do was
give in to the pressure Constantine was exerting and she
would be back in his bed. Again.

The restaurant was tiny and packed with customers but
Sienna's relief faded when the two dark-suited bodyguards
who had shadowed them since they'd exited the hotel suddenly disappeared and the proprietor led them to a private
courtyard. A lone table, which had obviously just been vacated by early diners, was in the process of being set.

Within seconds they were alone.

Girding herself for an unpleasant discussion that would spell the end of Ambrosi, Sienna took the seat Constantine held for her, but instead of launching into business, Constantine seemed content to relax and enjoy the meal. Listening to his casual banter with the proprietor who served them personally and observing his teasing charm when a small child ventured out of the kitchens to chatter shyly at them, she found herself gradually relaxing as well.

An hour later, after dining on creamy goat cheese and figs, followed by an array of fresh seafood including spicy fried squid, the local specialty, Sienna declined dessert.

Her tension snapped back as soon as they reached the enclosed gardens of the resort. The security team melted away once again and she found herself alone with Constantine. Warily, she studied a walled garden with its limpid ornamental pool. Nothing about this part of the resort was familiar. "Where are we?"

"My private quarters. I was about to offer you a nightcap."

Something kicked hard in her chest. Disappointment. "If this is a proposition, believe me, right now sex is the last thing—"

"What if I cleared the debt?"

His words were like a slap in the face, spinning her back two years to the scene in her apartment when Constantine had point-blank accused her of agreeing to marry him in order to guarantee the financial health of Ambrosi Pearls.

It had taken months but she had finally decided that if he didn't know who she was, or what was important to her, that was his problem not hers.

It was difficult to believe that she had ever been naive enough to imagine that he had fallen in love with her, that they had spent six weeks together making love.

Not making love, she corrected. Get it right. Having

sex. Doing exactly what they had done on his couch three nights ago in Sydney.

Constantine hadn't moved. He was simply watching her, his arms folded over his chest, utterly cool and in control. She was suddenly sharply aware that she was being manipulated.

He wanted a refusal.

He had deliberately goaded her in order to get one. Interesting.

Why ask if she would sleep with him for money now, and in such an insulting manner, unless he had finally realized that he had been wrong about her two years ago?

"Last I heard," she said quietly, "you weren't finding it that hard to get a date."

"I take it that's a 'no.'"

"Take that as a definite 'no.'"

"Would the answer have been different if, instead of a temporary arrangement, I'd proposed marriage?"

Bleakly, Sienna decided, that question hurt even more than the last. She scanned the garden in order to get her bearings and find the quickest route back to her room. "There's no point to this conversation since you didn't propose. But since you're so interested…" Hating the huskiness in her voice, she started toward an indentation in the wall that looked like a door. "If I ever do marry, the relationship and my husband will have to fit around my needs."

"I take it that means Ambrosi Pearls?"

A sharp thrill coursed down her spine when she became aware that Constantine had padded up close behind her. As she stepped deeper into the inky shadows that swamped the courtyard, the notion that she was not only being maneuvered but actively hunted, intensified. "Not anymore, since you're intent on relieving me of that particular burden."

Halting at the wall, she studied the door, searching for a way to open it. Like the problems in her life, there did not appear to be a simple answer.

"Interesting," he muttered, "that you should use the word burden. I would never have guessed that you craved freedom."

"Freedom. Now there's a concept." The thought of being free of the debt burden was suddenly, unexpectedly heady, even if it did mean the demise of the company.

Guilt for the disloyal thought fueled her irritation as she pushed at the door. It gave only slightly. Frustration gripped her. She was over being a victim, especially of garden designers. "Please tell me this opens."

Constantine reached down and released a small latch she hadn't noticed in the dark. His arm brushed hers, sending a small shock of awareness through her. Her frustration mounted, both at her knee-jerk response and the fact that the door swung open with well-oiled ease. She was certain that at some level, Constantine was enjoying this and, abruptly, she lost her temper.

Two more steps and the conversation would be over, for tonight. "Back to the hypothetical marriage." As she stepped past Constantine, she deliberately trailed one finger down the lapel of his jacket.

The gesture was intimate, provocative, a dangerous form of payback that registered in the silvery heat of his gaze. "If you are considering a proposal, like I said in Sydney, if the prospective husband just happens to have a healthy bank balance and a flair for financial matters, as far as I'm concerned the situation would be win-win."

Constantine controlled the fierce heat flowing through him as Sienna strode down the path that led back to the resort's main reception area. She mounted a set of stone steps, the champagne silk gown swirling around outrageously sexy high heels. For a split second, the garden lights glowed through the dress, outlining her long, shapely legs, giving the momentary illusion that she was naked.

As distracting as the thought of Sienna naked was, it was the image of her naked and wearing Medinian bridal jewels that was consuming him at that moment.

Constantine briefly acknowledged the security guard he had tasked with protecting Sienna as the man stepped past him and followed her at a discreet distance. There were no serious threats on Medinos but, after the stir she had caused by attending his hotel opening wearing bridal jewels, the paparazzi were bound to hear about it.

Added to that, Alex Panopoulos was here and on the hunt. Constantine didn't regard the Greek as a serious threat, but if he tried to approach Sienna, Constantine wanted to know about it.

When both Sienna and the bodyguard had disappeared from sight, he closed the courtyard door with quiet deliberation and locked it.

It had gone against all of his instincts to let her go, when what he'd really wanted was to cement his claim. But there would be time enough for that, and he knew if he touched her now he wouldn't be content with playing the part of a restrained lover.

He hadn't liked hurting her, but she had pushed him with the jewels and the dress. He had needed to see her reaction to his proposition and he had gotten the result he had wanted. Despite ruthlessly using his company's promotional event to target new sales avenues for Ambrosi Pearls, she had refused to sleep with him to save her company.

What he hadn't bargained on, ever since he had seen her at the funeral, was his own response.

Just days ago he had been certain of Sienna's involvement in her father's scam. But the second she had lifted her head and looked at him at her father's funeral, as if they were still lovers, he had been the one who had been unmasked. He had wanted her whether she was innocent or guilty.

He had studied all of the paperwork and Ambrosi Pearls' financials. There was no tangible link between Sienna and the money Roberto had siphoned out of his father.

Two years ago he had miscalculated. He was determined not to do so a second time.

He wanted Sienna, but as far as he was concerned there were now only two options. It was either strictly business, or bed.

Ten

Dawn streaked the horizon with shades of gold, purple and rose as Sienna walked to the largest of a network of tropically landscaped pools. Shivering slightly at the cool dampness of the morning—supplemented by the resort's sprinkler system, which jetted vaporized water into the air—she eased out of her sandals.

A faint movement caught her eye as she dropped her towel, key and sarong onto one of the resort's deck chairs. The bodyguard who had followed her to her suite the previous night was standing beneath one of the palms. Annoyed, but determined to ignore him so long as he kept his distance, she walked into the water.

She swam energetically for a few minutes then turned on her back to catch her breath. The snick-snick of the sprinklers had stopped, replaced by slow dripping as lush palms shed excess water onto smooth limestone paving.

The deep quiet of the early morning gradually sank in, mending the ravages of a mostly sleepless night.

Constantine had offered to clear Ambrosi Pearls' debt if she slept with him.

Taking a deep breath, she ducked and breaststroked the length of the pool underwater, using the discipline of the physical challenge to cool her escalating temper. When she surfaced at the opposite end her lungs were burning.

On a scale of insults, she guessed it wasn't any worse than the ones he'd leveled at her two years ago, but the fact that he still viewed her that way after all this time was infuriating. If she had wanted to marry money, she could easily have found herself a rich husband by now. She hadn't. Two years after their split, she had barely dated.

Unlike Constantine.

Which brought her back to the manipulation angle.

For reasons of his own, Constantine wanted her off balance. Given his stake in Ambrosi Pearls, the reason couldn't be a business one. He already held all of the cards in terms of money and power. Barring a miracle from de Vries, Ambrosi Pearls was at his mercy; whatever Constantine wanted to happen, would happen. All she could do was plea bargain for her family and the staff.

If it was anyone but Constantine she might assume he wanted revenge, except he could have had that two years ago. All he'd had to do was expose the scandal of her father's dealings and the press would have ripped her reputation to shreds. He had chosen not to do that, saving her that final humiliation.

She frowned, her thoughts going back to Constantine's proposition.

The fact that he had made an offer, couched in business terms, meant he would be prepared to pay, and that, she decided, made him insect material.

Feeling happier with her assessment of him, she swam another length, kicked toward the steps and walked out of the water, slicking wet hair out of her eyes.

Movement sent tension zinging through her. Not the security guy or Constantine. Alex Panopoulos was ensconced on the deck chair next to hers.

He pushed to his feet, her towel in his hands as she approached. "Do you usually swim alone?"

Sienna smiled coolly, her gaze missing his by a calculated few millimeters. "I swim for exercise, not company."

Predictably, he didn't let go of the towel when he handed it over, so that she had to engage in a miniature tug-of-war to pull it free.

Annoyed by the game, and feeling exposed in her bikini when he was fully dressed, she forced another cool smile. "Mr. Panopoulos, if you don't give me the towel, I'll walk back to my suite without it."

"Alex, please." With a shrug he let the towel go. "I was hoping you would agree to be my date at lunch."

"Sorry, I already have a date." She quickly dried off as Panopoulos persevered with a predictable stream of conversation then wrapped the sarong around her breasts.

A flash of movement caught her eye. Constantine, dressed in low-riding gray sweatpants and a soft, faded muscle shirt, as if he'd been jogging, was strolling toward her from the direction of her room. Realization dawned. Constantine's bodyguard had informed him that she had company at the pool.

Constantine nodded at Panopoulos, his greeting curt.

His gaze locked on hers. "Are you ready to go?"

Suddenly any male threat that Panopoulos posed seemed ridiculously tame. Panopoulos's face actually paled as Constantine collected her things.

Sienna scooped up the damp towel. "What took you so long?"

His hand cupped her elbow, and they were moving. She managed to pull free without making it look like a fight. Reflexively, she rubbed her elbow, which tingled with warmth. "Thanks for the rescue, but you don't have to take it this far. I can cope."

Sunlight glanced off the grim line of his jaw. "What did Panopoulos want?"

"That's none of your business."

"If he's bothering you I'll take care of it."

"The same way you deal with newspaper reporters?"

A glint of amusement entered his eyes. "No." Sienna was transfixed by an emotion she absolutely did not want to feel: a primitive surge of satisfaction because her man had stepped in and claimed her.

Her man. Her heart pounded once, hard. She must be out of her mind. She should resent Constantine's actions; she should be fighting with him. Instead her body was in the process of a slow, steady meltdown.

She stopped walking, forcing him to halt. "Why are you having me watched?"

"Not watched, looked after. A couple of the major tabloids have published speculative stories linking us romantically. And Panopoulos hasn't exactly kept his mouth closed about what he wants."

"I can deal with Panopoulos."

His gaze narrowed. "Like you did just then?"

A door slammed. Voices and laughter pierced the air, unnaturally loud in the morning stillness. Sienna was suddenly acutely aware that the sarong had soaked up the dripping moisture from her hair and her bikini and had become transparent where it clung.

Two young children barreled along the path, followed

by their parents. Sienna stepped aside to allow them passage. It was time to take some control back.

She held out her hand, palm up. "Sandals and room key, please."

Annoyingly, Constantine handed them over as if there wasn't an issue. She slipped her feet into the sandals, and wished she had thought to bring dark glasses. They did a great job of shouting "distance," which right now she desperately needed.

The rising sun shone directly in her eyes as she rounded a curve in the path, determined to put some distance between herself and Constantine. Because her feet were wet, her sandals kept slipping, making walking awkward.

Constantine easily kept pace beside her. "Be careful, those pavers are slippery."

"I'm fine."

In an effort to put more space between them, she edged sideways, and then she did slip.

Constantine's hand briefly closed on her arm, steadying her. "Why don't you ever listen?"

She jerked free and stalked the rest of the way to her door. "When you say something I'm interested in hearing, I'll listen."

"That'll be when hell freezes over, then."

The words were bitten out, but laced with an amused exasperation that, frustratingly, charmed her and made her want to bite back and bait him a little more.

Grimly, she fitted the key card in its slot. "You know what, Constantine? Maybe you should stop worrying about what I'm doing and get yourself a life."

"What makes you think I don't get exactly what I want?"

The low, sexy register of his voice froze her in place. Now was the time to back off, to step inside and politely close the door, but his gaze held her locked in some kind of stasis. She knew what it was; she had spent enough time analyzing why she had fallen so hard for Constantine in the first place. It was the alpha male thing; he took control and for reasons unknown, she responded. In this case he had dealt with Panopoulos as easily if he had been shooing a fruit fly away and she couldn't help but be impressed.

"I came over this morning to apologize. I'm sorry about the position I put you in last night, but I had to know. I also owe you an apology for what happened two years ago."

She blinked, struggling with the abrupt mental shift. Of all the scenarios she had gone over in her mind, she had never imagined that Constantine would apologize for their breakup. "What made you change your mind?"

"I did some research—"

"You mean you had me investigated."

"Call it what you like," he said flatly. "All of your financial dealings and business practices are straight down the middle. Roberto was the taker; you were the giver. Nothing in your pattern indicated that you would resort to fraud. And after what happened two years ago, and the fact that you had never tried to contact me again for money or anything else, I decided it didn't make sense that you were involved in this deal."

Sienna briefly saw red over the way he had arrived at his verdict. "Let me get this clear. Because I didn't ask you for money after we split up, I'm okay?"

A pulse jumped along the side of his jaw. "It's standard practice to run security checks on business associates."

"Tell me, did you have me profiled two years ago before you decided to date me?"

"Calm down," he said curtly, as if she was actually going to follow that order.

Fingers shaking with outrage, she started to tap in the

PIN that unlocked her door but before she could complete the sequence, he snagged the key card out of the slot and slipped it into his pocket.

"Oh, this is good. A repeat of the he-man tactics."

His brows jerked together. "What he-man tactics?"

She began to tick them off on her fingers. "The threat over my father's grave, holding me against my will in your car, forcing me to meet you the night after the funeral—"

"I didn't hold you against your will. We were in a supermarket parking lot. If you hadn't avoided me for four days, the meetings would have been conducted in a conventional business setting."

"I had no reason to want to see you. If you'll remember, the last conversation we had wasn't exactly pleasant."

"Which is why I'm apologizing now."

"Two years too late, and it's the worst apology I've ever heard."

His gaze glittered in the dim coolness of the portico that shaded her door. "Nevertheless, you're going to hear the rest of it. I tracked the loan payments. They were all deposited into one of your father's personal accounts, not Ambrosi Pearls' working account."

"That's right, one of Dad's gambling accounts, which was why I couldn't be sure the money wasn't winnings. If you knew that, why ask if I'd sleep with you for money, when you already knew I wouldn't?"

"You weren't involved in your father's loan scam, but that didn't mean you didn't know about it."

"So you tested me." Okay, she had expected that. She understood that a lot of women would be attracted to Constantine simply because he was so rich and powerful. But that didn't excuse him for thinking she could be one of them, or the fact that he still didn't get her.

She met his gaze squarely, which was a mistake, because Constantine's eyes were one of the most potent things about him. They pierced and held with a steady power that had always made her go weak at the knees. "Apology accepted, as far as it went, but I'd prefer that we just stuck to business. Like, for example, what time can we meet today?"

She knew about the official luncheon, because she had an invitation. There was also some kind of photo shoot for Medinos's most famous export, gold, scheduled for later in the day. "I've got meetings most of this morning, so I've slotted you in after lunch."

"Good, because I'm booked to fly out this evening." An early afternoon meeting would also give her the time she needed to meet with Northcliffe and hopefully wrap up the de Vries deal.

"I don't believe you personally wanted the money two years ago," he said abruptly. "What I could never accept was the fact that you gave your loyalty to your father and your company instead of to me."

"I was afraid you'd break the engagement if you found out, which you did, so I guess the lack of trust goes both ways."

His fingers tangled in her wet hair. "Two years ago," he muttered huskily, "I wasn't thinking straight."

Her stomach tensed against the tingling warmth of his touch. "Are you saying you were wrong?"

"I'm saying I shouldn't have let you go."

His answer neatly slid away from the admission she had wanted, but when his palm cupped her nape, a pang of old longing mingled with a raw jolt of desire shafted through her.

Eleven

Constantine's head dipped. Sienna had plenty of time to avoid the kiss, a long drawn out moment to understand that this was exactly the result she had wanted, and then his mouth settled on hers.

Her palms landed on his chest, curled into soft interlock. The hot scents of male and sweat filled her nostrils, triggering memories. Flash after hot flash of his long, muscled body against hers, the damp drag of skin, his hands on her hips, the intense pleasure she'd derived from every touch. The shattering intimacy of making love...

She went up on her toes, leaned into the kiss. A small sound shivered up from deep in her belly. He stepped closer, moving her back a half step until her spine settled against the cool barrier of the door. His hold was loose enough that she could easily pull free. One hand still cupped her nape, the other was spread across the small of her back, but, contrarily, having the choice granted her the freedom to stay.

Somewhere in the back of her mind she was aware that she shouldn't be responding to a man she had spent two years avoiding for a whole list of excellent reasons. Surrendering to him physically went against common sense and plain old-fashioned pride. But a reckless, starved part of her wasn't interested in reason and logic.

Her arms curled around his neck. The unmistakable firmness of his arousal pressed against her belly, sending a shaft of heat through her, and a fierce, crazy elation. Two years, and nothing had changed.

She still wanted him and she had no earthly clue why. For example, why didn't she feel this way about the occasional nice man she had dated since Constantine? Why hadn't she fallen into adoring lust with any one of the hundreds of bronzed, attractive stockbrokers and nine-to-five guys who littered Sydney's Central Business District?

She could have a pleasant, comfortable life with someone who actually loved her. A home, babies…

His mouth slid to her throat. The rough scrape of his jaw sent another raw shudder through her. Gulping air, she dragged his mouth back to hers.

The problem was she responded to Constantine in a way she didn't respond to any other man. It was depressing to think that she might actually be drawn to him because he was so difficult to handle, that after years of suppressing her own desires in order to save Ambrosi Pearls, she needed the battle to feel alive.

Lust was lust, it didn't impress her overly and it had never gotten the best of her before now. She was healthy, with a normal sex drive, but she was also ultrapicky. She didn't just like things so-so; they had to be perfect. Flowers had to be perfectly arranged, her accessories had to complement what she was wearing, otherwise she couldn't concentrate on anything but the fact that something was wrong, even if it was only one minor detail.

A natural extension of that pickiness was that the men in her life had to be right. They had to look right, smell right, feel right, otherwise she just wasn't interested.

Though he was too big, too experienced, too dangerous—nearly more than she could handle—Constantine did smell and taste and feel right, when no one else had ever come close.

His hand slid up over her waist and rib cage. The heat of his palm burned through the sarong as he cupped her breast and gently squeezed. The pad of his thumb rasped over her nipple. A sharp, edgy tension gripped her and for an endless moment her mind went utterly blank. His thumb moved in a lazy circle. The tension coiled tighter, and her mind snapped back into gear.

Oh, no. No way.

She pulled free, banging the back of her head against the door in the process. "I can't do this, not again. I need my key."

When he calmly handed it to her, she lodged it in the lock, tapped in the PIN and shoved the door wide.

She swiped up her towel, which she must have dropped at some point. "That kiss was a mistake. I'm here on business. I can't allow anything to mess that up."

"Don't worry, Ambrosi Pearls will be taken care of."

The breeze plastered the soft tank against the muscled contours of his chest. A resurgence of the hot, edgy tension that had gripped her when he had cupped her breast made her stomach tighten and her nerves hum. "What does that mean, exactly?"

He dipped his head and kissed her again, and like a quivering, weak-kneed fool she let him.

"Simple. I want you back."

Heart pounding, Sienna locked the door. After showering, she blow-dried her hair, applied makeup with fingers that were annoyingly unsteady, then checked her reflection: cream pants, cream camisole, Ambrosi pearl accessories. Cool, calm and classy, the exact opposite of the way she felt.

Constantine wanted her back.

He had said Ambrosi Pearls would be taken care of, although that didn't make sense because the one fact Constantine had always made clear was that he had no interest in committing the cardinal sin of mixing business and pleasure.

After collecting her sample case, she walked to Northcliffe's suite. Just minutes into the meeting, when Northcliffe discreetly checked the time on his watch, Sienna realized her sales pitch wasn't going well.

A short time later, Sienna replaced the sample case in the safe in her room and booted up her laptop. Stunningly, despite keeping her dangling for weeks and showing a good deal of interest, Northcliffe had declined to place an order.

Without a major deal in the pipeline, Ambrosi Pearls was officially in financial jeopardy. With no further sources of revenue, there was nothing to stop Constantine taking the company.

Still in shock at her utter lack of success, Sienna opened up her sheets of financials then put a call through to the company accountant. Sydney was eight hours ahead of Medinos, which meant that her early morning call came in midafternoon for Brian Chin.

After a terse conversation regarding their options—basically none—she asked to be put through to Carla.

Carla was predictably to the point. "Have you talked to Constantine?"

"Not yet, but he has indicated that he will look after the company."

"I'll bet."

They both knew that Constantine was entitled to take the company and break it up if he wanted; after all he had paid for it. If he allowed Ambrosi Pearls to keep trading, that was the best-case scenario.

What worried Sienna most now was that the heavily mortgaged Pier Point house and her mother's small apartment in town, which were both tied in with the company, would go. They had already sold the town house to meet debts. After everything her mother had been through, and in her present fragile state, the thought that she would literally lose everything made Sienna sick to her stomach.

"Did he give you any details about just how he's going to look after Ambrosi Pearls?"

Sienna's cheeks heated. "He didn't go into fine detail." Unless she could count the slow stroke of his fingers at her nape, the glide of his mouth over her throat...

"I'm getting subtext."

"We were...arguing."

There was a taut silence. "He is after you again. I saw the way he was watching you at the funeral. And he went with you to the house afterward. I mean, why was he there at all? Why didn't he just send his legal counsel?"

Sienna finished the call, but Carla's words had sent a small unwelcome shock wave through her. Since she had closed the door on Constantine she had kept herself busy, specifically so she couldn't think, because every time she considered his statement that he wanted her back, her brain froze and her hormones kicked in.

The thought that he had wanted her back before he had landed in Sydney added a layer of calculation to his motives.

He had apologized. Not in a way that made her feel good, but in a factual, male way that told her he was telling the truth. He believed she hadn't been involved in the current scam, but not that she couldn't be an opportunist when it came to money.

He wanted her back, but she couldn't go back into a relationship when she knew Constantine still didn't trust her. Something was going to have to change. He was going to have to change, and she didn't know if that was possible.

The bedside phone rang while Sienna was changing for lunch. Her stomach performing somersaults, because it was most likely Constantine, she picked up the receiver.

It was Tomas.

"Good morning," he murmured in his precise English. "Constantine is busy with meetings until twelve and has asked me to brief you."

"Let me get some paper." Sienna tossed the floaty floral dress she planned to wear over the bed and found a pad and pen in the top drawer of the bedside table. She picked up the phone, expecting to jot down numbers and legal details.

There was a brief pause. "I'm afraid you misunderstand. The briefing concerns lunch."

"Lunch?"

"That's correct."

Tomas followed up with a clipped list of do's and don'ts that sounded like something out of a Victorian diary. Modest dress was essential, with a discreet décolletage and a length preferably below the knee. Low-key makeup and jewelry were advised.

There was a small pause. "There will be a large press contingent at the product launch. Mr. Atraeus has requested that you adhere to his requirements."

The receiver clicked gently in her ear. Sienna listened to the dial tone for several seconds before putting the phone back on its rest.

She stepped out onto her private patio and took a deep breath. Unfortunately, her patio garden, aside from a gorgeous view of Ambrus, also framed the Atraeus fortress where it commanded the headland and a good deal of the island.

Not good.

Her temper still on slow burn, she stepped back inside, repacked the floral dress and shook out a sleek white Audrey Hepburn–inspired sheath that came to midthigh and extracted the flower pearl set from the sample case.

After the disappointment of the meeting with Northcliffe, she had no desire to drink champagne and smile and pretend that everything in Ambrosi Pearls' world was fabulous. Now that the company's fate was sealed, she would have preferred to stay out of the public eye and away from the press.

She had even less desire to follow Constantine's orders.

Minutes later, she checked her hair, which she'd pinned into a smoothly elegant chignon. The style was sophisticated and timeless, a good match for the opulent pearls at her lobes and throat.

The hair and the jewelry were perfect; the dress, however, failed to meet the criteria Tomas had outlined. The scoop neckline displayed a tantalizing hint of golden cleavage, the dress was short enough to reveal the fact that she had great legs, and in no way was the dress inconspicuous.

She sprayed herself with perfume then, on impulse, tucked a delicate white orchid from the tabletop arrangement behind one ear.

The flower transformed the look from sexy sophistication to something approximating bridal.

Satisfied with the result, she slipped into strappy white heels that made her legs look even longer, picked up a matching white clutch and left the room.

Constantine wouldn't miss the message, and that was fine with her. The sooner he realized she would not allow him to control her, the better.

Twelve

Lunch was an elegant affair, with a marquee on the lawn, a classical quartet playing and a well-known opera diva singing.

As Sienna strolled through the garden she spotted Constantine, who was wearing a gauzy white shirt over dark close-fitting pants. He glanced at her. She smiled coolly at a spot somewhere over his left shoulder and pretended she hadn't seen him.

A number of willowy models, dressed as brightly as birds of paradise, swayed through the crowd, weighted down with Atraeus gold. Sienna stiffened as she recognized two prominent gossip columnists sipping champagne, one of whom had relentlessly defamed her following the breakup.

She paused by a heavily guarded display cabinet showcasing exquisite gold and diamond jewelry. The reason for the two armed security guards was clear. Aside from the small fortune in jewelry displayed, the centerpiece was a pale pink baguette diamond ring that glittered with a soft fire. Very rare and hugely expensive.

"Sienna?" The editor of a prominent women's magazine paused beside her, smiling brightly.

Sienna braced herself to make polite, guarded conversation, ignoring a hot pulse of adrenaline when she realized Constantine was walking directly toward her.

The editor briefly studied Sienna's pearl necklace. "I love the pieces you're wearing." She made brief notes about the pearls and Ambrosi Pearls' upcoming collection.

When she moved on, Sienna's attention was drawn back to Constantine who had been waylaid by a pretty woman dressed in an elegant pants suit. She recognized Maria Stefano, the daughter of a prominent European racing magnate, because she had recently been photographed with Constantine at a high-profile charity function.

Maria wound her arms around Constantine's neck and leaned into him for a cooing hug. Constantine's expression as he gazed into her upturned face was amused, bordering on indulgent, and the sudden tension in Sienna's stomach intensified.

Realization hit her like a kick in the chest. She needed to walk someplace quiet and bang her head against a brick wall, because she was jealous of Maria Stefano.

The reason she was jealous was just as straightforward: she was still in love with Constantine.

Her chest squeezed tight. For a long moment she couldn't breathe, then oxygen whooshed back into her lungs, making her head spin. Constantine was single, fatally attractive and hugely wealthy. It was a fact that if he wanted a woman, he usually got her. Over the past two years he had dated a number of women, but until now they had mostly been blank faces and bodies. It had been easy to ignore the gossip because he had never had a steady girlfriend.

A photographer aimed a camera their way. Maria slid her arm around Constantine's waist and posed. By then several other cameras were clicking. Seconds later, Constantine excused himself, cutting the photo session short.

When he reached her side any trace of indulgence was gone. "You don't have to be jealous."

Sienna concentrated on the jewelry in the case and tried to ignore her body's automatic reaction to Constantine's piercing gaze, the clean masculine scent of his skin. "I am not jealous."

"Then stop worrying about other women."

Heat and a totally male focus burned in his eyes. If she'd had any doubt about his intentions or the lovemaking in Sydney, they were gone. He really did want her back.

Although, she was certain that a long-term relationship or marriage were not on Constantine's agenda. All he wanted was a wild, short-term fling.

That he expected her to jump back into bed with him after the sneaky way he had used her financial situation to maneuver her made Sienna so furious she had to unclench her jaw before she could speak. "Why don't we just go to your office now and talk about the loan agreement your father and mine cooked up and see where that takes us?"

Wariness flickered in his gaze. "Not yet," he said mildly. "Unless you came all this way to hand me a check."

"If there was a check, I would have mailed it."

"That's what I thought, in which case we'll stick to the schedule and discuss finances after lunch."

A camera flashed almost directly in her eyes. The photographers who had been so interested in Constantine and Maria were now concentrating on her.

A waiter offered her a glass of champagne. She refused

the drink, although for a split second tipping the chilled contents down Constantine's shirtfront was an irresistibly satisfying image. She had a better idea.

She half turned, brushing close to Constantine as she continued her perusal of the jewelry in the display case.

His gaze dropped to her mouth, and a small hot thrill shot through her. She had been so busy concentrating on Constantine's power and dominance, she had forgotten that she wielded her own power, that two years ago, for a short time at least, he hadn't been able to resist her.

His gaze rested briefly on the white orchid in her hair. "Damn, what are you up to?"

She kept her expression bland. "If you don't want to talk about business now, that's fine by me, but I'm in the jewelry trade and I am here on business. I'd like to take a closer look at the contents of this cabinet."

One hand was casually propped on the display cabinet behind her. To a casual observer they must have looked cozily intimate. For long moments, she thought Constantine was going to refuse, that she had overplayed her hand with the bridal theme—that he could see the sudden crazy plan she had formulated.

Just when she thought he would refuse, he nodded at one of the security guards, who stepped forward and unlocked the case.

Feeling wary but exhilarated, because what she was about to do was risky, she examined the array of beautifully crafted jewelry. Before she could change her mind she selected the largest ring, the pink diamond baguette. As engagement rings went, it would one day make some woman blissfully happy. "Four carats?"

Constantine's gaze was coolly impatient. "Maybe five."

"But then diamond rings aren't your thing, are they?"

He had never given her one, because their engagement had ended before the ring he had commissioned was ready.

After two years the lack of a ring shouldn't matter but in Sienna's opinion, and her mother's, not presenting a ring when he had proposed had been a telling factor.

According to Margaret Ambrosi and Aunt Via if a man didn't humbly offer a ring when he proposed—the best possible ring he could afford—that was a *sign*. The ring wasn't about money; it was about sacrifice. If a man truly loved a woman then he would be more than happy to demonstrate his love to the world by putting his ring on her finger.

To make matters worse, the lack of a ring had somehow made their weeklong engagement seem even more insubstantial. To Constantine the exquisite jewel was just a pretty, expensive trinket, without meaning beyond the calculated profit margin. No sentiment and definitely no emotion involved.

They were almost completely encircled by media now and the security guards weren't happy. Jaw taut, she held the ring out to Constantine. When his hand automatically opened, she dropped it into his palm. She registered the stir of shocked interest, his flash of surprise the moment he logged her not-so-subtle message that this time she wouldn't accept anything less than marriage.

The cool metal of the ring burned Constantine's palm. As his fingers closed around the band, his annoyance—at Sienna for wearing a dress that had every red-blooded man drooling, for wearing the same set of pearls she'd had on when they had made love on his sofa—dissolved.

The reporters and the buzz of conversation faded. He felt as if an electrical charge had just been run through his system, lifting all the fine hairs at his nape.

The bridal white, the pearls and the ring were a statement

He had gotten the message—loud and clear.

Grimly, he decided he should have expected that she would hit back. In a moment of clarity, he realized that if he had wanted a woman who would allow herself to be dictated to, he would never have chosen Sienna. The CEO of a company that would have been highly successful if Roberto Ambrosi hadn't drained its profits. Sienna was formidable and a handful, and in that moment he was clear on one fact: she was his.

Instead of replacing the ring in the case he clasped her left wrist and slipped the ring neatly on to her third finger. "I would have chosen the white diamond," he murmured.

Shock registered in Sienna's gaze as he slid his arm around her waist, curving her into his side. "Looks like the wedding's on."

His expression controlled, Constantine made brief eye contact with the head of his security team as cameras flashed and the questions started.

Keeping Sienna clamped firmly to his side, he forged a path through the reporters. Moments later, with the help of security, they were clear.

Sienna sent him a stunned look. "Why did you do that?"

"The gesture was self-evident."

She made a strangled sound.

Constantine's jaw tightened. "After what you pulled, both last night and today, no one will believe you didn't angle for marriage."

"You didn't have to compound the issue by putting the ring on my finger."

"It was a spur-of-the-moment thing."

Unlike the past two years which had been ordered and precise, and without any discernible excitement. Seven days ago, he had been okay with that. As the Americans would say, all his ducks had been in a row. Now he wasn't sure if he could live without the chaos. "What I'd like to know is why you decided on the bridal theme?"

For a moment, he was caught between amusement and frustration and a definitely un-PC impulse that would ensure they were front-page news.

The glass doors of the hotel slid open.

Sienna threw him a suspicious glance. "Where are you taking me?"

Constantine felt like saying "To bed," but managed to pull back from that precipice. "The manager's office."

"Oh, goody," she muttered. "I've been wanting to check out all day."

Ignoring startled looks from hotel staff and guests, Constantine hustled Sienna down a corridor and into the large executive suite he had been using as his office, and kicked the door closed behind him.

Sienna spun to face him. "That was a press announcement out there."

He leaned against the door and folded his arms across his chest. "You wanted to play, those are my rules. Last night you turned up at my hotel opening wearing what looked like Medinian bridal jewels. On Medinos that amounts to an engagement announcement."

Her cheeks heated. "I've already told you, I had no idea the jewels we designed on the basis of Sebastien's drawing were wedding jewels! How do you think my family will feel when they open up tomorrow's newspapers and discover we're now supposed to be engaged?"

Her dark gaze held his and another one of those sharp, heady thrills burned through him. The past two years had definitely been flat. "You want me to issue a denial about the engagement?"

"It wouldn't be the first time." She yanked the ring off

her finger and dumped it in his palm. "And in the process it's entirely possible that this time you could look bad."

Given the string of stories dating back to the first broken engagement and the fact that she was presently grieving for her father, make that very bad. Worse, he decided, he would look like a man who couldn't make up his mind or control his woman.

Turning on her heel, Sienna paced to the French doors, which opened out onto a patio. A shadowy movement, visible through the sheer curtains that filtered the overbright sun, stopped her in her tracks.

Constantine dropped the ring in his pocket and strolled behind the large mahogany desk that dominated the room. "If you're thinking of making a break for it, I wouldn't advise it. That could have been a security guard, but more likely it's a reporter trying to get an exclusive through the windows."

Her gaze snapped back to his. "Any publicity generated will be brief. Without a wedding, the story will die a natural death. Just like it did last time."

For a long, drawn out moment silence vibrated between them. Time for a change of tactic.

"All right," he said calmly. "Let's talk. As it happens, now is the perfect time."

He gestured toward one of the chairs grouped to one side of the desk.

A tension he hadn't been aware of eased when Sienna finally moved away from the French doors and took one of the seats he'd indicated. Picking up the briefcase he had deposited in the office earlier in the day, he extracted a set of documents and slid them across the glossy desktop.

Sienna frowned as she skimmed the first sheet. "I don't understand. I thought this would be a straightforward transfer of shares to cover the debt."

She returned her attention to the contract. Overhead a fan slowly circled, with a soft, rhythmic swishing.

Too tense to sit, Constantine took up a position in front of the French doors, standing in almost the same spot that Sienna had, unconsciously blocking at least one exit. He frowned when he realized what he was doing. He guessed, in its crudest form, the paperwork was another form of exit-blocking.

Sienna skimmed the final page of the document. He logged the moment she found the marriage clause.

Shooting to her feet, she dropped the contract on the desk, her eyes dark with shock. "This is a marriage deal?"

"That's correct." Grimly, Constantine outlined the terms, even though he knew that Sienna, with her background in law, would have no problem deciphering the legalese.

Part of the deal was that she signed the transfer of the lease on the old pearl facility on Ambrus and the water rights to The Atraeus Group. In return, her family would retain a minority holding in Ambrosi Pearls. All debts and mortgages would be cleared, including those on the family house in Pier Point and Margaret Ambrosi's city apartment. Constantine had undertaken to reinvest in the company and retain all jobs. With the income from their shares, all three Ambrosi women would be able to live comfortable, debt-free lives.

Sienna shook her head. "I don't understand. If you need a wife, you could have any number of women. You could marry someone who has money—"

Relief loosened the tension that gripped him as he had braced for a refusal. He had known she wanted him, but until that moment he hadn't known whether or not she would agree to marriage. "I want *you*."

"Two years ago you threw everything away because of a loan."

"Two years ago I made a mistake."

He had a sudden flash of the night they'd first made love, the roses and the champagne, the sweetness and laughter when he'd let her seduce him. The chemistry between them had been riveting. He had spent two years without Sienna. Despite his crammed schedule and the fact that he had been absorbed with the challenge of running The Atraeus Group, it suddenly felt like he'd spent two years in a waiting room. "There is nothing complicated about what I want."

Shaking her head, she picked up her clutch, which she'd placed on the desktop. "You and I and marriage... It doesn't make sense."

He covered the distance between them and drew her into a loose hold. She had plenty of time to pull back, and he was careful not to push the physical intimacy, but it was a plain fact that, right now, touching her was paramount. He needed to cement his claim.

Taking the clutch from her, he placed it back on the desk and linked his fingers with hers. This close he could smell the flowery sweetness of her perfume, the faint scent of the orchid in her hair. "We share a common heritage. Marriage made sense two years ago."

"Two years ago we had an ordinary, normal courtship."

"Which is precisely why this should work now."

He lowered his mouth to hers, keeping a tight rein on his desire. One second passed, two. Her lips softened beneath his. She lifted up on her toes, and in agonizingly slow increments wound her arms around his neck and fitted her body to his. His arms tightened around her, exultation coursing through him at her surrender.

His cell phone buzzed, breaking the moment. Curbing

his frustration, Constantine released Sienna to answer the call.

Tomas. He strolled to the window and listened, his attention split as Sienna picked up the contract and studied the pages, her profile as marble-smooth and remote as a sculpture.

She wanted him. He was almost certain that she loved him, but he was aware that neither fact would guarantee her acceptance, and he wasn't prepared to compromise. When serious money had entered his parents' relationship equation, his mother had used the wealth to finance her exit from their lives. His father had remarried, but his wealth had also opened the door to a number of stormy extramarital relationships. With the debacle of his previous engagement to Sienna, Constantine had decided that the one thing he required in his marriage was control.

The contract was cold-blooded, directly counter to the way he felt, but if they were going to do this, he needed clear-cut terms. He would not live the way his father had done, at the mercy of his desires, or allow Sienna to run roughshod over him. This time there would be no gray areas and no hidden agendas.

Sienna's head jerked up as he disconnected the call. The orchid, he noticed, had dropped from her hair and lay crushed on the floor.

Her gaze met his, outwardly calm and cool but dark with emotion. "How much time do I have to think this over?"

Constantine slid the phone into his pocket. "I need a decision now."

Thirteen

Sienna lowered herself into the chair she had previously vacated, the leather cool enough against the backs of her thighs to send a faint shiver down her spine. "What happens if I say no?"

Constantine's gaze was unreadable. "I can have another, more straightforward document drawn up if you don't sign this deal."

The alternative document would be the one she had expected, taking everything—the business, her mother's house and apartment. It would, no doubt, make a large number of Ambrosi employees redundant, and could spell the end of Ambrosi Pearls altogether.

Constantine had made his position clear. There was chemistry enough to smooth the way, but this wasn't a courtship, or even a proposal. It was a contract, a marriage of convenience.

For a moment, after the softness of that kiss, she had

hoped he would say something crazy and wonderful like, "I love you."

Although the time for those words and that moment had been two years ago and they hadn't ensured happiness.

The flowery romantic love that had originally swept her off her feet was long gone, and she wasn't sure she wanted it back. The illusion of love had hurt.

Despite the pragmatism, hope flared. Maybe Constantine didn't love her, but this time, despite the enormity of what her father had done to the Atraeus family, he had fought for her.

Instead of abandoning her to his legal team, he had stepped in and protected her and her family from bankruptcy proceedings and the press. He had also gone to great lengths to protect and care for her mother and make sure she retained an income and her dignity. That counted for a lot.

Sienna aligned the pages until they were neatly stacked. Two years ago she had frozen like a deer in the headlights. She had let her father's actions dissolve her chance at happiness.

Her chin firmed. She didn't like the businesslike approach to something as personal and intimate as a marriage, but she acknowledged that business was Constantine's medium. The explanation for a contract like this, which practically corralled her with obligations to her family, to Ambrosi Pearls and to him, was so that Constantine could feel secure that she was tied in to the marriage. If he needed the extra assurance, that meant she really did matter to him. She didn't know if this would work, but she would never find out if she didn't try.

She took a deep breath. "All right."

Constantine didn't try to kiss her, for which she was grateful, he simply handed her a pen.

When they had both signed the documents, he called in a witness, one of the hotel receptionists. It was all over within minutes.

Constantine's phone buzzed as he locked the documents back in his briefcase. He answered his cell then checked his watch. "I need to be on-site with the contractors on Ambrus in an hour."

She picked up her clutch purse feeling faintly giddy at the leap she had taken. She needed food, and she needed time alone to come to terms with a future that just minutes ago had seemed wildly improbable. "I'll wait here."

"Oh, no, you won't." His jaw was grim. "You're coming with me. Now that we are officially engaged, I'm going to make sure you don't get another opportunity with the press."

Heat blasted off the enormous skeletal structure that was the construction site on Ambrus, shimmering like vapor in the air as the helicopter touched down on a huge slab of concrete.

Hot gusts from the rotors, peppered with stinging dust, whipped at her face and hair, as Constantine helped her out of the chopper. Sienna, who'd had just enough time to change into casual clothes and sneakers, grabbed her brief-case, which she had refused to leave behind.

Constantine would be busy with the contractor who was managing the construction of the hotel complex for a couple of hours, which suited her. There was an office, a modern concrete bunker she had spotted from the air, where she planned to crunch some numbers and catch up on some paperwork. If she found herself with time on her hands, she could always take a walk along the exquisite jewel-like bay.

Clearly, this wasn't a part of Ambrus that had ever been

used for anything more than grazing goats, nevertheless, it was beautiful and from a family history point of view any part of Ambrus interested her.

Anchoring dark glasses on the bridge of her nose, Sienna ducked to avoid the rotors. Constantine's arm clamped around her waist, tucking her into his side as he hustled her beneath the rotating blades. Disorientation hit her along with a wave of heat as she adjusted to his hold.

Ever since she had agreed to the marriage she had been off balance and a little shaky, although Constantine hadn't given her time to think. Ever since they had left the hotel's office, he'd kept her moving. She'd only had bare minutes alone, and that time had been pressurized, because she'd had to change clothes and pack her briefcase in time to make the flight.

She stepped off the concrete pad. Her pristine white sneakers sank into coarse sandy grit and were instantly coated. Automatically, she lengthened her stride, stepping out of Constantine's loose hold, but he kept pace with her easily, underlining the fact that they were now a couple.

Her cheeks burned at the knowledge, although no one in their right mind would attribute her flush to anything but the intense heat. Already her clothes were clinging to her skin and she could feel trickles of perspiration running down her spine and between her breasts.

Behind them the engine note of the chopper changed, the pitch higher, as if the pilot was preparing for takeoff. Sienna brushed whipping tendrils of hair out of her face as the helicopter did lift off then veered back toward the coast. "If that was our ride, how do we get out of here?"

By her reckoning, at this end of Ambrus, they were forty miles at least from Medinos. Not a great distance as the crow flies, but complicated by the barrier of the sea.

Constantine, who had walked on a few steps, calmly

waited for her to catch up. In faded jeans and leather boots, his eyes remote behind dark glasses, he no longer looked like a high-powered business executive but as much a part of the wild landscape as his warrior ancestors must have been. "Don't worry about the transport. I've taken care of it."

Sienna watched the helicopter turn into a small black dot on the horizon and the disorientation hit her again. "I could be crazy to trust you."

Out here there were no taxis and, according to Constantine, no cell phone service until they installed a repeater on one of the tall peaks in the interior. Telephone and internet communication was limited to the satellite connection in the office.

He held out his hand. "You've trusted me this far."

Sienna laced her fingers with his, the sense of risk subtly heightened by the casual intimacy. No matter how right it felt to try again with Constantine, she couldn't forget that just hours ago she had been uneasy about his agenda and certain that no matter how intense the attraction, there was no way a relationship could work.

The office was modern, well-appointed and wonderfully cool.

While Constantine was immersed in a discussion with the site manager, Jim Kady, Sienna appropriated an empty desk. She hadn't yet called either her mother or Carla, because Constantine had asked her to wait until they could inform both of their families. Although with the media stir following Constantine's announcement, she needed to call either that evening or first thing in the morning.

Setting her briefcase down on the desk, she eased out of her sneakers and shook the excess grit into a wastepaper basket. Padding through to the bathroom in her socks, she grabbed paper towels, dampened them then grabbed an extra handful of dry towels. When she returned to the office, Kady had left and Constantine was propped on the edge of the site manager's desk, taking a call.

She sat down, cleaned her shoes and brushed off her socks, which had a brownish tinge. She became aware of Constantine watching her, obviously amused by her perfectionist streak.

"You'll pay for this," she said lightly, trying to defuse the mounting awareness that she was alone with Constantine for the first time since they had signed the agreement.

His expression was oddly intent and ironic. "That I do know."

Her breath caught in her throat and her heart began to pound. It was a weird moment to understand that he liked her quirkiness, that he didn't just want sex and a controllable wife; he wanted her.

The sound of rotor blades filled the air as a helicopter skimmed low overhead.

Constantine checked his watch. "That'll be the engineer."

Relief flooded her. Rescue and reprieve. And the transport was back.

Just over two hours later, when Constantine's meeting was wrapped up, he walked back into the office.

Sienna kept her head down, ostensibly working on Ambrosi Pearls' figures, although it was little more than doodling with numbers. She would no longer be in charge of the major investment decisions, but after years of financial stress and buoyed by the heady opportunities ahead, it had been a pleasurable way to pass the time.

The heat hit her like a blow as she stepped outside with Constantine. In the distance the helicopter, which had been sitting on the pad, lifted into the air taking the group of suits attached to the contracting firm back to Medinos. Sienna checked to see if there was a second helicopter, just in case she had missed hearing it come in.

The pad was bare.

Constantine halted beside a four-wheel drive pickup truck that looked like a carbon copy of the truck Kady had parked outside the office, except this one had a bright blue tarp fastened over the bed.

When Constantine opened the passenger-side door, indicating they were driving somewhere, she dug her heels in. "I thought we were going back to Medinos."

"We are, but not just yet. While we're here, I wanted to show you the old pearl facility."

Which meant he had planned this. "If I don't get back soon, I'll miss my flight out."

"The company jet is on the runway at Medinos. You can catch a flight out on that when we get back."

His hands settled at her waist, and suddenly there was no air. He muttered something in Medinian. "I wasn't going to do this yet." Bending, he captured her mouth with his, the kiss hot and hungry and slow.

She froze, for long seconds caught off balance by the ruthless way he was conducting their so-called engagement and her knee-jerk response.

His mouth drifted along her jaw, she felt the edge of his teeth on her lobe. A small smothered sound escaped from her throat. His lips brushed hers again and her arms closed around his neck as she lifted up against him, returning the kiss.

He lifted his head. His forehead rested against hers. "Are you coming with me?"

Sienna let out a breath. This time he was asking, not demanding, but she was also suddenly aware that in spending time alone with Constantine she was agreeing to much more than a sightseeing tour.

The panic she'd felt in the office hit her again. She felt as jittery as a new bride, but she had agreed to marry him and it wasn't as if they hadn't made love before. "Okay."

Feeling distinctly wobbly, she climbed into the truck. Setting her briefcase down on the floor, she fastened her seat belt.

Constantine swung behind the wheel and put the truck in gear. Despite the fact that she had agreed to go with Constantine, the feeling of being herded was strong enough that she was about to demand he drive her back to the mine office when the VHF radio hissed static. Constantine answered the call and the moment passed.

Several minutes later the construction site was no longer visible. There was a rooster tail of dust behind them and the heat shimmer of the rugged island wilderness in front.

Time passed. At some point, lulled by the heat and the monotonous sound of the truck motor, she must have fallen asleep. Straightening, she brushed hair out of her eyes and checked her watch. A good thirty minutes had passed.

She frowned as she studied the road, which was now little more than a stock road running beside a wide, deep green river.

At periodic intervals along the narrow ribbon of road, marker poles had been placed indicating floodwater levels, in places a good meter above the road. There was further evidence of a previous flood and occasional washouts, where portions of the road had been eaten away by the destructive power of the river.

"How far are we from the pearl facility?" The road they were following appeared to be getting narrower.

"Five miles."

Five miles there, then a good thirty miles back to the construction site.

Minutes later, after driving through a deep gorge, Constantine picked up the radio handset again, tried the frequency then set the handpiece down. "That's it. We're out of radio range for the next few minutes. Now we can talk."

His voice was curt as he outlined the business plan for Ambrosi Pearls. He had taken a look at the structure and none of the staff would go, although that would be open for review. Given that the business had been tightly run and had only stumbled because of the debt load imposed by her father, redundancies weren't an option at this point. "Ambrosi Pearls stays in business." There was a brief, electric pause. "But you have to go. Lucas is taking a block of shares. He'll be stepping in as CEO."

Blankly, Sienna wrenched her gaze from Constantine's profile, her mind fixed on his statement that she would have to go.

"Let me get this straight, you want me out of the company completely?"

"That's right, and I'm not asking."

She stared at the stark line of the horizon, rugged hills and more rugged hills threaded by the road they were presently following. She had been braced for demotion. She had not expected to be fired.

She peeled her dark glasses off and rubbed at the sudden sharp ache in her temples. She could feel Constantine studying her, the ratcheting tension.

Although she should have expected this.

Constantine lived on Medinos, therefore it would be difficult for her to remain based in Sydney.

Constantine slowed to a crawl as he drove across a stretch of road that looked like it served a double purpose as a streambed during the wet season. "We signed a contract. You agreed to be my wife."

Her jaw set. "At no point did I agree to give up my job."

Ambrosi Pearls was her baby. She had nursed it through bad times and worse, working crazy hours, losing sleep and reveling in even the smallest victory. She knew every aspect of the business, every employee personally, and their families; they were a tight-knit team. Despite the stress and the worry the company was hers. She was the captain of the team. Ambrosi Pearls couldn't run without her. She felt the cool touch of his gaze.

"I want your loyalties to lie with me, not Ambrosi Pearls. We'll be based in Medinos. Running an Australian business won't be an option."

She stared at the road unfurling ahead, the blinding blue intensity of the sky, the vastness of the sea in the distance. "You run any number of hotels and companies from Medinos."

"Each one has a resident manager. In this case it will be Lucas."

He was right—she knew it—but that didn't make relinquishing Ambrosi Pearls any easier. From childhood she had grown up with the knowledge that, love it or hate it, she would run the family business. "I'm good at what I do. I've studied, trained—"

He braked, allowing a small herd of goats to drift desultorily off the road. "I know how focused you've been on Ambrosi Pearls. No one better."

"Plenty of women juggle a career and marriage."

"Ambrosi Pearls will not be part of this equation."

"Why not?"

His gaze sliced back to hers. "Because I refuse to take second place to a briefcase filled with sales orders."

Sienna jammed her dark glasses back on the bridge of

her nose, abruptly furious at Constantine's hardheaded ruthlessness. "You still don't trust me."

Less than an hour ago she had let him kiss her. He had manipulated her into agreeing to a lot more, despite knowing he was going to sack her while they were driving. "Looking after Ambrosi Pearls has never been just about business. It's part of my family. It's in my blood."

Gaze narrowed, she stared directly ahead, searching for a place where Constantine could comfortably turn the truck around. "I've changed my mind. I want to go back."

"No. You agreed to this."

"That was before you fired me."

"We're spending the night at a beach house up ahead. I'm taking you back in the morning."

Her head snapped around. "I did not agree to that. I do not, repeat, do not, want to spend the night with you. Take me back to the construction site. There must be some kind of regular transport service for the workers. If I'm too late to catch whatever boat or helicopter they use, I'll use the satellite phone in the office to call in my own ride."

"No." His voice was calmly neutral. "The beach house is clean, comfortable and stocked with food."

She could feel the blood pounding through her veins, her temper increasing with every fiery pulse. "Let me guess, no landline, no cell phone network, no internet connection…just you and me."

"And no press, for approximately twelve hours."

With movements that were unnaturally calm, given that she was literally shaking with fury, she unlatched her briefcase and retrieved her cell. She stared at the "no service" message on the screen. Any hope died.

The pearl facility was sited on the western side of the island, tucked into a sheltered bay directly behind the range of hills that was presently looming over them, blocking transmission. "Turn the truck around. Now."

She repeated her request that he turn around immediately.

When he ignored her for the second time, she studied the tough line of his jaw, the dark glasses that hid his eyes, and gauged her chances of yanking the key out of the ignition.

"I don't want to spend the night in some beach house," she said, spacing the words. "I don't want to drive one more mile with you. I'd rather crawl across the island and die of thirst, or swim to Medinos. And if you think I'm going to have sex with you, you can think again. Think dying or rabid thirst, because either of those two things will happen first."

The stare he gave her was vaguely disconcerted, as if he was weighing up which parts of her statements she would actually carry out. It was then she realized that he really did think he was still going to be having sex with her.

He turned back to the road, his jaw set. "We're almost there."

The landscape had changed, flattening out as they neared the coast. Blunt outcroppings smudged with grayish-green scrub and the occasional gnarled olive tree dotted the roadside.

He negotiated another bend and suddenly they were driving alongside the deep, green river again.

Her frustration escalated. Apart from throwing a tantrum, she was almost out of options—and she didn't do tantrums. She liked coolness and precision—pages of neat figures, relationships that progressed logically. She liked forward planning because she liked to win.

Briefly, she outlined plan B. Drive to a place where she could get cell phone service—there had to be a viable high point on this island somewhere—and call in a helicopter. Out here, with the primitive lack of any telephone or power lines, it could land virtually anywhere. If Constantine did what she asked, she wouldn't take this to the police or the newspapers. But if he kept driving all bets were off, and she would sue his ass.

Constantine had the gall to laugh.

A red mist actually swam before her eyes. Her hand shot out and grasped the wheel. He was momentarily distracted while she lunged at the key.

Any idea that she could get out of the truck and make it to a high point on her own was just that, a wild idea. All she wanted was to jolt Constantine out of his stubborn mind-set, stop the vehicle and make him listen.

Constantine jerked her hand off the wheel. Not that that was any big deal, because the maneuver was only a distraction while she grabbed at the elusive prize of the key. Unfortunately, when she had lunged forward, the seat belt had locked her in place, so she'd had to regroup and try again, which had cost her valuable time. Even then her fingertips could only brush the key.

Constantine said something hard and flat. Her head jerked up, not so much at the word, but at the way he'd uttered it.

She saw the washout ahead, which had gouged a crescent-shaped bite out of the road, a split second before the front wheel dropped into the hole. If Constantine had had his full attention on driving, he would have negotiated the hole. A floodplain fanned out on the driver's side. He could have detoured for fifty meters without a problem.

Constantine swung the wheel and gunned the motor, but with the ground crumbling under the rear left wheel there was no way he could pull them back on an even keel.

With a lurch, the truck tilted further.

There was a beat of silence, because Constantine had achieved what she had been trying to do and had turned the engine off. For an endless moment they teetered on two wheels then, with a slow, lumbering grace, the truck toppled sideways.

Fourteen

The distance from the road to the river below wasn't horrendous. From the vehicle it had looked tame, just another eroded riverbank, softened by time and not even particularly steep. But, like the moment when a roller coaster paused on the edge of a drop, no matter how small, the distance suddenly seemed enormous.

Sienna's seat belt held her plastered against the seat as the truck made a clumsy half revolution. Her glasses slid off her nose and a dark shape tumbled past her jaw—her briefcase. The vehicle rocked to a halt. They had stopped rolling, but they had ended upside down, hanging suspended by the seat belts. And they were in the river.

For a heartening moment they bobbed, the murky waterline changing as the truck settled lower. The light began to go as they were almost completely submerged by tea-colored water, tinted, she realized, by the mud that had been stirred up when the truck had disturbed the riverbed.

"Are you all right?"

She turned her head and stared at Constantine. He had a welt on his cheekbone, but otherwise he was in one piece. Apart from the fact that the truck had turned into a submarine and there was something trickling across her scalp—at a guess, blood, which meant she must have banged her head—she was good to go. "Just show me the exit sign."

"Good girl."

The truck was stationary, which meant the roof was sitting on the bottom of the river. That indicated that the depth was shallow, probably not even deep enough to cover the truck fully, but since water was hosing in at various points, getting out was a priority.

A sharp metallic click drew her attention away from the swirling mud and she realized that Constantine had been talking in a low voice. She forced herself to pay attention.

Constantine had already unclipped his seat belt. Using the steering wheel as a handhold, he lowered himself to the roof, which was now their floor, and reversed his position so that he was upright, his back and shoulders wedged against the dash. To do so he had to slide right next to her, because the steering wheel and the gear shift made maneuvering his big frame in the limited space of the cab even more difficult. There was no way he could stand upright.

Constantine leaned across her. She realized he was checking out her door. "The roof crumpled slightly when we went over. Not much, but enough that the doors won't open, so we're going to have to go out through the windows."

He unsnapped her seat belt and caught her as she fell, torpedoing into the deepening puddle of water. With her nose squashed against one rock-hard thigh, she hooked her fingers into the waistband of his jeans and awkwardly jackknifed in the confined space while he kept a firm grip on her waist, holding her steady. She ended up plastered against him from nose to thighs, his arms clamped around her like a vice and with the back of her neck jammed against the edge of the seat. But at least she was finally up the right way, which was a relief, although with her head in the darker floor cavity, the feeling of claustrophobia had increased.

"We're going to have to swim for it, but that shouldn't be a problem since we both know how good you are in the water."

Was that sarcasm? But with water creeping up her ankles she couldn't drum up an ounce of righteous indignation.

Constantine reached across her. She realized he was groping for the window which, luckily, was a manual wind-up type and not electric.

She tried to shuffle sideways, allowing him more room. In the process the top of her foot nudged against a hard object—her briefcase.

She had an instant replay of the sleek, black leather case flying around the cab—the probable cause of the stinging on her scalp. But the injury wasn't what obsessed her in that moment. The accident, stressful as it was, had had a strange effect. Her fury had zapped out of existence and the tension that normally hummed between them was gone. For the first time in two years, stuck upside down in a cab with Constantine as he took control in that calm, alpha way of his, she felt content and almost frighteningly happy.

It was a strange time to realize that despite the constant battles, at a bedrock level she trusted Constantine, and that two years ago when everything had gone wrong this was what she had needed from him.

"You're going out first," he said quietly. "I'll follow."

"No problem." Now that the mud had settled she could see that they were only a couple of feet from the surface. The biggest issue would be the few seconds wait while the cab filled with water. The moment most people would panic would be when the water gushed in. The important thing was to stay calm and hold her breath while the cab filled, because the last she wanted was to swallow a mouthful of river water.

"I'm going to unwind the window. Once the cab is full, you'll have to squeeze out the window. Are you good to go?"

Her head was throbbing a little, but she still felt pumped. Constantine's gaze was inches from hers. With water creeping up her legs and the muscular heat from his body blazing into her, if she hadn't been so at odds with him, she might have given into a *Poseidon Adventure* moment. "Just a second."

She bent her knees and slid down the front of his body. "Don't get any ideas."

She felt around in the water. Her fingers closed around the briefcase handle.

"Leave that."

Leave her laptop underwater? "No. I can use it as a flotation device."

"You can swim like a fish. You don't need a flotation device."

Sienna's head jerked up at his tone, connecting sharply with the back of the seat. A stab of pain shot through her. She had somehow managed to reinjure the same spot, which was now aching. She met his glare with her own version of a steely look. "I don't see why I should lose something I love just because you think it's a good idea." And with any luck the briefcase would be waterproof enough that the laptop would survive.

"I wonder whose idea it was to 'lose' the truck?"

The dryness of his tone flicked her on the raw.

Maybe the briefcase shouldn't be a sticking point, but suddenly it very palpably was. She had lost her company and her career, there was nothing she could do about that, but the briefcase was *hers*. "I'm happy to take the blame for the truck. Just don't blame me for the fact that you haven't gotten around to repairing your road."

"Why did I ever think this was viable?" Constantine jerked her close and pressed a brief, hard kiss on her mouth.

Adrenaline and desire shot through her. Constantine's gaze locked with hers and she had another moment, one that made her heart simultaneously soar and plummet. Her head was stinging and she was angry at the way he had all but kidnapped her, but those considerations were overridden by one salient fact.

No matter what he did, how badly he behaved, she still wanted Constantine. And not just in a sexual way. Her problem was that she wanted all of him—the overbearing dominance and the manipulative way he had pressured her into going into the wilderness with him so he could fire her then keep her prisoner until she forgave him. She wanted the aggravating challenge of his cold, ruthless streak and take-no-prisoners attitude, the flashes of humor. And last, and by no means least, she really, really wanted the heart-pounding sex.

"What now?" he growled, although that didn't fool her. He wanted her, too, and no amount of bad temper could hide that fact.

"Nothing," she snapped back. "As you can see I'm ready to go. I've been ready for ages."

A bare second later water flooded into the cab. The swamping flow would have shoved her sideways but Constantine held her firmly anchored against him. Closing her eyes and holding her breath, she counted and waited until the cold pressurized flow stopped. She opened her eyes on eight. The cab, now filled with water, was dimmer than before, although sunlight shafted through the windows.

Keeping a firm grip on the case, she levered herself out of the window, and kicked to the surface, into blue sky and hot sunlight.

She gulped air and treaded water while she got her bearings. The truck was completely submerged, the only sign of its presence in the river a muddy streak where silt and dirt stained the water. A raw gash on the bank marked the spot where they had gone off the road, but that, she realized was receding.

The current was carrying her downstream at a steady pace. Crumbling banks, eroded by time and scoured by flash floods, rose on either side of her. Despite the sunlight, the water was icy, but that wasn't her biggest problem. Constantine still hadn't surfaced.

Sucking in a breath and, yes, using the case as a flotation device, she kicked toward shore. She could swim against the current, but she would get back to the truck faster by getting onto dry land and jogging back.

Seconds later, her feet found the bottom of the river. Slipping and sliding on rocks, she slogged toward the shore, scanning the smooth green surface as she went. It was entirely possible that Constantine had surfaced for air then gone back down to the truck to retrieve something—maybe the radio set—and she had missed that moment. When she had surfaced she had been too busy hanging on to the briefcase to notice.

Setting the case down she jogged toward the gash in the bank that was now the only marker for the place the truck had gone in, since the muddy streak in the water had cleared. Simultaneously, Constantine surfaced from the now dimly visible shape of the truck, a pack in one hand.

Sienna used the strap of the pack to help pull him to shore. When they stumbled onto the riverbank she dragged the pack out of his hands, dropped it to the ground and checked him out for injuries, relieved when she couldn't see any blood. "Why didn't you surface straightaway?"

He slicked dripping hair back from his face and jerked his chin at the pack. "First aid. Food and clean water. And a portable radio, if it stayed dry."

Explosive anger burned at the back of her throat. Despite his practical reason for staying under and the fact that he had obviously felt confident he could hold his breath for all that time, it didn't change the fact that he could have been in trouble. "That pack wasn't in the cab."

Which meant it had been secured on the truck bed, underneath the flatbed canopy. Instead of following her to the surface he had stayed underwater, holding his breath while he unlaced the tarp, swam beneath it and retrieved the pack. With the swift-flowing current anything could have happened. "I thought you were trapped."

His hands closed around her upper arms, rubbed against her chilled flesh. "It's okay, babe, I had a knife. I cut the canopy open. There was no way I could have gotten trapped."

Babe? Something snapped inside her. "Don't you dare do anything like that again."

Maybe she was overreacting, but the thought that something could have happened to Constantine made her go cold inside. For several seconds she had been forced to consider what life would be like if she did lose him. She hadn't known how much that would matter to her.

She was in love with Constantine. She had to face the fact that if she still loved him after the past two years then it was an easy bet that she would continue to love him, regardless.

She didn't know how long she would feel this way. Maybe sometime in the dim, distant future, whatever it was that sparked her to respond to him would fade and she would love someone else. She was certain love was possible, but she didn't know if she would ever be desperately, hopelessly in love again.

An emotion that made her heart stumble flashed in his gaze. He muttered something in Medinian and hauled her against him. Her arms clamped around his neck as his mouth came down on hers.

Heat radiated from him, swamping her, and the kiss pulled her under. For long seconds she drifted, still locked into the expression she had glimpsed in his eyes. The truth he had hidden from her for two years—that he wasn't either remote or emotionally closed down, that as much as she needed him, he needed her.

He lifted his mouth and she could breathe again, but it wasn't oxygen she wanted. This time there was no thunder and lightning, no thick darkness pressing down, hiding motives and intentions. Her fingers slid into his wet hair and pulled his mouth back to hers. The passion was white-hot and instant.

She found the buttons of his shirt and tore them open. Seconds later, she felt the rush of cool air as he slid her wet, clinging shirt off her shoulders. A sharp tug and her bra was gone. He pulled her close, the skin-on-skin contact searing. The uncomplicated relief of being held by the man she loved spiraled through her as she lifted up on her toes and deepened the kiss.

His fingers pulled gently at the pins in her hair, destroying the remnants of her chignon so that wet strands tumbled around her shoulders. She found the fastening of his jeans and tugged, then they were on the ground. For long minutes, between heart-stopping kisses, she was consumed with buttons and zippers and the breathless humor of constructing a makeshift bed with discarded clothing.

Another drugging kiss and her arms coiled around Constantine's neck, pulling until he ended up on top of her, and suddenly the humor was gone. Despite being in the water for longer than she had been, heat radiated from him, swamping her. The rumpled, wet clothing beneath was rough against her bare skin, but the discomfort slid away as her hands found the satiny muscles of Constantine's back and she stretched out against the smooth, sleek length of him.

His gaze locked with hers as with infinite gentleness their bodies melded, the fit perfect. For long moments they simply stayed that way, soaking in what they hadn't had time for in Sydney, the slow intimacy, the hitched breaths and knowing glances.

Warm, melting pleasure shimmered through her as they finally began to move together, their breath intermingled, their bodies entwined. Past and present dissolved as the burning intensity finally peaked and the afternoon spun away.

Long minutes later, Constantine rolled onto his back, pulling her with him so she lay sprawled over his chest.

Sienna cuddled close, ran her palm absently over one bicep, stroking the pliant swell of muscle. He moved slightly, shifting his weight. She adjusted her position, making herself more comfortable.

In that moment she faced a small detail that, caught in the maelstrom of emotion and urgency, they had both chosen to ignore. This time they hadn't used a condom.

The moment had been primal and extreme, but the fact that Constantine could have made her pregnant didn't terrify her. She had wanted him inside her, touching that innermost part of her.

His eyes flickered, his gaze found hers. She bent down and kissed him, her hair a damp tangled curtain enclosing them. His hands slid up her back, tightened on her waist and she was lost again.

The rising breeze roused Constantine. He hadn't gone to sleep, and neither had Sienna. Like him, she had been content to lie quietly, her breathing settling into an even rhythm.

"We're going to have to move." His skin was darkly tanned and used to the hot sun, but Sienna with her creamy skin and honey-gold tan would burn.

Regret pulled at him as she eased out of the curve of his arm and snatched up an armload of wet clothing. The skittish alacrity with which she draped their clothing over warm boulders then walked into the river informed him that her thoughts were running parallel to his. They had made love without a condom, twice.

It wasn't something he had planned, nor would he ever force this situation on any woman, but now that it had happened he had to reassess and act.

A child. He went still inside at the image of Sienna round and pregnant. Sienna with his baby at her breast.

Raw emotion grabbed at his stomach, his chest. Until that moment he hadn't realized how powerful lovemaking could be, or how imperative it was to him that Sienna was the mother of his children.

Sienna had always been attractive to him, almost to the point of obsession.

Almost, but not quite.

Two years ago he had been able to control his involvement. To a degree, he admitted grimly. When he had discovered that Sienna had known her father was using their engagement to leverage a loan, he had been able to step back. But at some point between their lovemaking in Sydney and now he had crossed a line.

That shift had happened when Sienna had walked into his hotel ballroom wearing what he had thought were Medinian bridal jewels. In that moment he had wanted every promise inherent in the intricate weave of the bridal jewels: purity, passion and commitment.

Rising to his feet, he followed Sienna into the water. Despite the possessive urge to keep her close, he was careful to allow her space and not push any further than he already had.

Ducking down, he rinsed his hair. Water streamed down his shoulders as he surfaced just in time to see Sienna wading to shore.

By the time he walked out of the water, she was wearing her shirt, which had already dried in patches. With swift movements, he dried off with his shirt and pulled on his underwear and jeans, then replaced his shirt on its rock to dry some more, along with his socks and boots. The jeans were still damp, but the weather was so hot they would dry almost as quickly while he was wearing them.

Sienna, who had already finger-combed her hair and tied it in a neat knot, unlaced her sneakers. "That can't happen again. Making love without a condom is crazy."

"I didn't exactly plan to have unprotected sex."

His gaze narrowed when she calmly ignored him in favor of turning her jeans and socks over and aligning everything with military precision. She selected a rock, sat down and started brushing grit off her sneakers. He could feel his temper slipping then he finally got it. Sienna was a perfectionist; it had always been one of the things he had liked about her. He had even thought it was cute on occasion, although it periodically drove him crazy. Like now.

But suddenly the reason she fussed and tidied was clear. It was her way of coping when she was stressed or worried. She had done it in the office this afternoon and she was doing it now, which meant the cool distance wasn't a brush-off; it was simply a means of protecting herself.

Relief dissipated some of his tension as he walked over to Sienna. Crouching down, he cupped her face and gently kissed her. "I'm sorry I didn't use a condom, but given the way things were and the fact that I didn't have one, there was no avoiding it this time. Next time we make love I'll take care of the protection. There are condoms at the house. They were delivered along with the food."

Her gaze flashed. "You really did plan this."

"You knew as well as I did the minute you climbed in that truck what was going to happen. I asked, you agreed. I didn't make you do anything you didn't want to."

This time she avoided his gaze altogether, but he didn't need the eye contact to know exactly what was going through her mind.

Frowning, he straightened. Any woman would worry about an unplanned pregnancy. But if Sienna was pregnant, as far as Constantine was concerned, the situation was cut-and-dried. They would be married within a month.

Fifteen

Sienna studiously avoided Constantine's gaze as she finished cleaning her shoes. Heat and silence shimmered around them, broken by the cooling sound of river water sliding over rocks.

She was lacing one sneaker, when Constantine crouched down in front of her and picked up the other one.

His hand encircled her ankle and something snapped. Images flickered in her memory: the way she'd melted the first night they'd met when Constantine had crouched down and fitted her missing shoe to her foot. Not a glass slipper exactly, just a black pump with black beads, but the moment had been incredibly, mind-bendingly romantic.

She swiped the shoe out of his hand. "Don't."

She sucked in air, tried to breathe. Maybe she was being stubborn and picky, but she didn't want those kinds of gestures unless he really did love her. Pulling at the laces, she loosened them off enough to put the sneaker back on her foot.

Constantine frowned as his gaze skimmed critically over her. "You're bleeding. You should have told me."

She touched her scalp. There must be a cut because there was dried blood, but it was so small she had difficulty finding it. "It's nothing, a scratch."

He unfastened the pack and tipped the contents out on the ground, one of which happened to be a pack of emergency supplies. Standard issue, she guessed, for anyone who worked out at the construction site. The other was a first aid kit.

While he was sorting through the supplies Sienna went down to the river to rinse the blood out of her hair.

When she returned, Constantine appeared to be busy tinkering with the portable radio. Dragging her gaze from the powerful line of his back, Sienna finished dressing except for the still-damp bra, which she folded and slipped into her jeans pocket. She strolled a few steps down the rocky beach, staring at the wild beauty of the landscape. With every moment that passed the commitment she had made in making love to Constantine without protection seemed more and more foolhardy in light of his glaring lack of any kind of emotional declaration.

A flicker of movement caught her eye. Constantine was by her briefcase.

Her brows jerked together as he picked it up and sneakily carried it up the bank. Out of sight.

Her temper shredding, she stormed up the bank and retrieved the briefcase. She didn't know what it was with Constantine and her things. He wasn't just satisfied with taking her company and her job; now he didn't want her to have her briefcase.

He frowned. "You don't need that. You'll only have to carry it."

"I do need it, and it's no problem carrying it." And if he

wanted to take it off her now, he would have to pry it out of her cold, dead hands.

His gaze narrowed, glittering with an edgy frustration that sent a zingy sensation down her spine. "Jewelry samples and order forms are the last thing you need out here."

She felt herself blushing at the confirmation that he had recognized her sample case back in her hotel suite. She stared at his muscled chest and a small, red mark on his shoulder she could remember making. She felt herself grow warmer. "It's not a sample case. For your information it's a portable office."

"The same thing in my book."

For a taut moment she thought he was going to say something further then he turned back to the assortment of tools he had assembled on the ground.

Still tingling with the heady knowledge that Constantine wasn't as distant and controlled as he seemed, she took the briefcase back to her rock, sat down and unlatched it. Water had seeped in, wetting the order forms but, because her laptop was zipped into a soft case inside the briefcase, it was still bone-dry.

She set the damp forms down on the ground to dry, extracted the laptop, powered it up then closed it down. She packed it away, and tidied her appointments diary and the jumbled mess of pens and pamphlets then placed the damp order forms on top. They were no longer any use, but since there wasn't a trash can out here, she would have to keep them until she could find one.

When she had finished restoring order to the briefcase, she slipped her cell phone out of her pocket and tried that, without much hope. As she'd thought, it was as dead as a doornail.

Constantine strolled over with a first aid kit. He sat down on a rock in front of her and leaned close, sandwiching her between his thighs. She was suddenly overwhelmingly aware of the broad expanse of his chest and just how physically large he was.

He tilted her head and she found herself looking directly into his eyes. His face was close enough that she could study to her heart's content the intriguing dark flecks in his irises, the red welt on his cheekbone that was rapidly discoloring into a bruise.

He cupped her face, his hold seducingly gentle. "If you get pregnant, we'll talk about it. Until then, we'll go back to using protection."

Sienna edged the briefcase away from his booted foot, ignoring his irritated frown. "Assuming there is going to be more sex."

"How likely are you to get pregnant?"

She drew in an impeded breath, suddenly floored by the thought that she could be pregnant, right this second. It was documented history that Ambrosi women got pregnant at the drop of a hat. They were psychotic power freaks when it happened, but certifiably fertile.

She did a quick count. "There's a possibility."

More than a possibility.

His thumb brushed across her mouth sending a hot little dart of sensation through her. "I'll leave you alone for now, if that's what you want. Now stay still while I take a look at that scratch on the side of your head."

Obediently, she tilted her head so he could examine the area. He took his time smoothing her hair out of the way then used some antiseptic wipes from the first aid kit.

"Ouch."

His mouth quirked at one corner. "Don't be a sissy."

"That's easy for you to say. You're not the one who's bleeding."

"The cut is small. It's hardly life-threatening."

"Then I don't know why you're bothering with the first aid routine."

He didn't reply, just angled her head again, pinched the wound together with his thumb and forefinger, which made it throb and sting, and smoothed on a small butterfly strip.

She stared at the welt on his cheekbone as he packed the first aid kit away. The bruise, which had started to turn a purplish color, made him look faintly piratical. "How did you get that?"

His gaze was slitted against the sun making him look even more dangerous. "The same way you got that cut on your head—from that damn briefcase."

She purred inside and inched the briefcase closer to her leg. She almost felt like patting it. Good briefcase, it had never meant to hurt her; it had been after Constantine.

He pushed to his feet. "The house isn't far, but we need to get moving. I checked the radio, and it still works, but we're out of the transmission area so we'll have to wait for the helicopter, which will be out to pick us up first thing in the morning."

Sienna watched as Constantine repacked the supplies and finished dressing.

He passed her a water bottle. Wordlessly, she drank. With the risk of giardia and other contaminants she hadn't drunk any of the river water, as tempting as the notion had been.

Constantine stored the bottle in the pack and held out his hand. "I'll take the briefcase."

"No. I'll carry it."

There was an explosive silence, but when she stole a sideways glance at Constantine she was certain his mouth was twitching.

The beach house, which had been less than two miles

away from where the truck had overturned, was not a cottage so much as a multilevel statement in design.

Decks merged into the side of a striated cliff and overlooked a windswept beach. Inside, the floors were glossy, the ceilings high. Huge plate-glass windows provided an unimpeded view of the sea.

Constantine pointed out the large adjacent bay, which held the old pearl facility, but by then the light was fading. Sienna could make out the tumbled remains of a building and little else.

Constantine touched a switch and air-conditioning hummed to life, instantly cool against her overheated skin.

Feeling dusty and tired, Sienna did a quick tour of the kitchen. Stainless-steel appliances were hidden behind lacquered cabinets, and a state-of-the-art oven, large enough to cater for a crowd, took pride of place. She opened a cabinet door and found a gleaming microwave and, on a shelf beneath it, an array of small appliances. "This place is fabulous. It doesn't look like it's ever used."

"It's a family retreat, but since we have to spend so much time overseas, it isn't used often. There are bedrooms upstairs and on this floor."

Constantine crossed the broad expanse of the living area, which was tastefully decorated with comfortable leather couches, and pushed open a door.

She followed him into the broad hall, which had several rooms opening off it. After a quick walk through, she chose a room with floaty white silk draperies.

Constantine showed her the bathroom, which was fully stocked with an array of products, including toothbrushes and toothpaste. "There's fresh underwear and clothing in the dresser if you want it. Freshen up, I'll go and organize some food."

After showering and changing into fresh underwear

and a thin cotton robe she'd found hooked on the back of the bathroom door, Sienna gathered up her soiled clothes and carried them through to the living area.

The aroma of a spicy casserole, which evidently had been prepared and left in the fridge, drew her to the kitchen. Constantine must also have showered, because his hair was damp and slicked back. He had also changed, pulling on a pair of clean cotton pants and a thin, gauzy white shirt.

He showed her where the laundry room was. She put her clothes and his in to wash, then walked back to the kitchen.

They sat out on the deck, a casual option that appealed more than the formality of the dining room, and ate the traditional Medinian dish followed by slices of juicy mango. The sun sank slowly, throwing shadows and investing the ocean with a soft, mystical quality that caught and held her gaze for long minutes.

When the sun finally slid below the horizon, the air temperature dropped like a stone. After the burning heat of the day, cold seemed to seep out of the rocks, raising gooseflesh on her skin. The night sky was unbelievably clear, the stars huge and bright and almost close enough to touch.

Sienna offered to clean up and make coffee, abruptly glad to escape the romantic setting and the growing tension. She stiffened when Constantine put on soft music and sat beside her on the couch but, when he didn't do anything more than drape his arm along the back of the couch, she finally relaxed.

After what had happened that afternoon, she had been prepared for a passionate interlude she wasn't sure she could resist. Instead he seemed to be doing exactly what she had asked: backing off and giving her some time.

Exhaustion pulled at her as she listened to a Beethoven adagio. But she could not forget what had happened that afternoon. She had to wonder if she was pregnant.

Her hand moved, cupping her belly. Constantine's gaze followed the movement as if he was entertaining the exact same thought.

She was suddenly acutely aware of her body.

The first shock of the idea had passed. Having a child would definitely narrow her options, but the notion of having a baby had taken firm root.

As if he had read her mind his hand smoothed down one arm, his thumb absently stroking her. The touch was pleasant rather than sexual, as if he was aware of her turmoil and wanted to soothe her.

Gradually, she relaxed against him. She was dropping into a delicious dark well of contentment when his voice rumbled softly in her ear.

"If there's a likelihood that you're pregnant, then we should get married soon."

Her eyes popped open. Suddenly she was wide-awake.

He hadn't proposed, either back at the resort or here.

Maybe there was no need for an actual proposal. Strictly speaking, that formality had been taken care of by the contract, but that didn't change the fact that she would have liked one. Although demanding that would let him know exactly how vulnerable she was about their relationship. "When did you have in mind?"

"A week. Two at the most."

"I'll talk to Mom and give you some dates." It was a surrender. The only thing left to extract from her was an admission that she loved him, but she would hold back on that for as long as she could.

Maybe denying Constantine that final victory was childish, but she was afraid that if she surrendered emotionally he would no longer feel he had to fight for her. If Constantine deemed his battle won, she could lose any chance that he would eventually love her.

He wouldn't walk away this time, so the outcome would be much worse—they could end up locked together in a loveless marriage. She may have given up on the romantic fantasy of having him fall in love with her, but gaining a measure of love, however small, was vitally important.

"That's settled then," he said quietly. "I'll take care of the arrangements as soon as we get back."

Shortly after daybreak the *chop-chop* of a helicopter split the air as it set down on a concrete pad a short distance away.

Fifteen minutes after boarding the helicopter, they set down at Medinos's airport. Less than an hour later a car, driven by Tomas, deposited them at the *castello*.

Constantine had arranged to have her things delivered to the *castello* from the resort, so as soon as they arrived she was able to change into fresh clothes.

When she was dressed in a cool, ice-blue summer shift that ended midthigh, she slipped on sandals and strolled through broad, echoing hallways and vaulted rooms, looking for Constantine. When she didn't find him, she checked the ultramodern kitchen.

Classical music had been playing, but in the lull between CDs she heard voices. She walked down a hallway, which led to the front entryway and a series of reception rooms.

As she padded closer, she noticed a door that had been left slightly ajar. The conversation, originating from that room and naturally channeled by the acoustics of the hall, became clearer. She recognized the distinctive American accent of Constantine's legal advisor, Ben Vitalis.

"...good work getting the water rights transferred so quickly..."

Her fingers, which had closed around the brass door-knob, froze as Vitalis's voice registered more clearly. "...if Sienna had contested the estuarine lease, the marina project would have stalled indefinitely. We would have lost millions in contractor's kill fees."

There was a pause, the creak of a chair as if Vitalis had just sat down. "...Clever move, inserting the marriage clause. Even if she tries to contest the transfer of the lease, under Medinian law the rights will revert to you. Where are we with the loan?"

"The loan agreement is cut-and-dried."

The deep, incisive tones of Constantine's voice hit Sienna like a kick in the chest.

She went hot then cold. The reason Constantine had proposed a marriage of convenience in the same contract that settled her father's fraudulent debt was suddenly glaringly obvious. Somehow her father had messed up Constantine's development plans. Constantine had wanted to ensure that his marina went ahead unchecked and she had succumbed to his tactics with ridiculous ease.

A painful flood of memories swamped her—the clipped conversation that had ended their first engagement two years ago, Constantine's detachment after their lovemaking in Sydney.

She could forgive the way he had gone about seducing her. Even knowing she was being maneuvered, she had been helpless to resist because she had known with every cell of her body that the desire was heart-poundingly real. But this level of calculation was not acceptable. She would have to be willfully blind, deaf and dumb not to understand that a third, even more profound rejection, was in the works.

"Okay, then…" There was a click as if a briefcase had been opened, the slap of a document landing on either a table or a desktop. "Cast your eye over the child custody clause."

Feeling like an automaton, Sienna pushed the door wide and stepped into the room just as Vitalis flicked his briefcase closed and rose to his feet. Constantine's gaze connected with hers and her heart squeezed tight. She had wanted to be proved wrong, to discover that she'd gotten the conversation wildly out of context, but in that moment she knew she hadn't.

Nerves humming, she stepped around Vitalis, picked up the document lying on the desk and skimmed it.

Seconds later she literally felt the blood drain from her face. She didn't care about land or money. She cared that Constantine had manipulated her over the water rights. It was a betrayal of a very private kind that cut to the bone because it emphasized that he didn't simply want her; she was part of a business agenda. Even knowing that, she would have gone through with the marriage. But the children she might have were a different matter.

She didn't know what it was like to bear a child, but even without the physical reality of a child in her arms, she knew how fiercely she would care about her babies.

Vitalis had prepared an amendment to the marriage deal, granting Constantine custody and rights for any children. If she walked out on the marriage, she would be granted limited access to her children, but she could never take them with her.

Before he even knew she was pregnant, should she decide to leave the marriage, Constantine had arranged to take her babies from her as coolly and methodically as he had taken Ambrosi Pearls and her career.

She transferred her gaze to Constantine. "Did you actually think that I would sign this?"

Constantine pushed to his feet. Vitalis had already retreated, melting out of a side door she hadn't noticed.

"It's a draft Ben put together. You weren't supposed to see it yet. I intended to discuss options with you next week."

Options.

She could feel herself closing up, the warmth seeping from her skin. She had known she would have a struggle breaking through the protective armor of Constantine's business process. He thought she was tied to Ambrosi Pearls, but her focus on the family business was nothing compared to his. It was possible that she was even partly responsible for the way he was handling their relationship—as if it was a business merger—because of what had happened two years ago. "But this is the deal you want?"

His expression was guarded. "Not...exactly."

Not the answer she needed.

Blankly she struggled to readjust her internal lens. "I've spent two years beating myself up because I agreed to marry you knowing that my father had organized a finance deal with yours. That was such a crime."

She replaced the pages on his desk. She was toweringly angry and utterly miserable. Marriage was personal, intimate. When she had said she would marry Constantine, she had done so imagining that he could feel something real and special for her, that if it wasn't love right now it would grow to be one day. She had been operating on hope.

The exact opposite of this cold agreement.

Constantine pushed to his feet. "I want a wife who is committed to marriage and family."

She registered that he was still dressed casually in the

jeans and loose shirt he had been wearing when they had left Ambrus. The reminder of the hours they had spent together on the island was the last thing she needed. "So you drew up a contract."

"It wasn't as cold-blooded as that. We're sexually compatible. We share a lot in common."

With the bright glare of the sun behind him throwing his face into shadow, she was unable to discern emotion either way, and in that moment she desperately needed to see something. "From where I'm standing, the only true bond we share is a seven figure debt."

In a blinding flash, being part of Ambrosi Pearls ceased to be important. For years she had been consumed with saving the company. The struggle had taken every waking moment, but with the safety of the company employees and her family assured, she didn't have to continue fighting. None of them did. Constantine would fight the battle for them. She could let go, step back, because Constantine was more able to manage her family's company than she would ever be.

But the last thing she wanted was to step into a relationship that was defined by a maze of legal traps. "And to think, I let myself fall for you all over again."

Secure in the glimpses of the old Constantine, with whom she had fallen in love. Secure in the illusion that she had some womanly power and a measure of control.

Something shifted in his gaze. "Sienna…I didn't mean to hurt—"

"No. Just control, because that's what works for you. Control me, control any children, control your emotions." There would be no messy divorce or outrageous property settlements, because the bottom line was clear-cut. "You told me that you usually get exactly what you want. I guess that really is a marriage of convenience and two—"

Blindly, she flipped pages and checked the fine print, but couldn't distinguish individual words because her eyes were filmed with tears. "Or is that three children?"

Constantine speed-dialed Tomas as Sienna walked out of his office and bit out orders, sheer, blind panic making him break out in a cold sweat. Sienna was leaving the *castello* and the island. As much as he needed to keep her with him, he knew that if he tried to physically detain her, he would lose her forever.

The fact that he had considered holding her in the *castello*—in effect, perpetrating the kidnapping she had accused him of when he had taken her to the beach house on Ambrus—demonstrated his desperation.

When Sienna had registered the contents of the child custody clause he had understood the mistake he had made, that no amount of financial or legal pressure would make him first in Sienna's life, or bind her to him the way he needed her to be if she didn't want to be there.

In that moment he had recognized her; he had seen the steady fire and strength that had always unconsciously drawn him. He had seen flashes before—in Sydney after they had made love, in the walled garden of the hotel when she had thrown his blundering attempt to make her choose between Ambrosi Pearls and him back in his face.

She had said she had fallen for him and in that instant he had known that was the reason she had agreed to marriage, not the financial breaks.

That moment had stunned him. He realized he had been first in her life all along. It was his approach that had been flawed. He had been the one who was focused on business.

His only break was that she hadn't mentioned the marriage clause. They were still engaged, on paper at least.

Tossing the agreement in his briefcase, he strode upstairs to his suite and threw clothes into an overnight bag. Tomas would make sure Sienna couldn't get on a regular flight out of Medinos even if that meant he had to buy every empty seat on the outgoing flights.

Bleakly, he recognized that when it came to Sienna, the bottom line had never mattered. The first time he had laid eyes on her he had tumbled. He had known who she was, had recognized her instantly, and he had been entranced. The problem was he hadn't believed she would simply want him. In his own mind he could still remember what it was like to have nothing, and how lacking in popularity he had been then.

Money had changed their lives. Maybe he was overly sensitive, but he knew that when women looked at him now they saw his wealth. Like it had for his father, money had been the dominant factor in almost every relationship. He had made the mistake of assuming that because Sienna needed money, that she would need him.

He had been wrong.

Now, somehow, he had to make up for his mistake, to convince her that they still had a chance.

He didn't care what it took. He just wanted her back.

Tomas rang back. The private jet was fueled; there were no longer any available flights out of Medinos. If Sienna wanted to leave today, it would have to be on the Atraeus jet.

Constantine hung up and returned downstairs to collect the keys to the Maserati. She wouldn't like it. That was an understatement. Sienna would hate the forced proximity, but he knew with gut-wrenching clarity that he couldn't afford to let her go completely. Every second she was away from him would widen the gulf he had created between them.

Thirty minutes later, Constantine parked the Maserati at

the airport, completed the exit details and walked through to his private hangar. Tomas had informed him that Sienna was already on board.

During the flight Sienna barely acknowledged him, choosing to either sleep, or feign sleep, most of the way.

Constantine forced himself to remain calm. This was damage control. If he didn't fix the mistakes he had made they were finished, and he had made a number of serious errors.

Given the choice, he wouldn't have used a marriage deal. The document had filled him with distaste, but when it had come to dealing with Sienna and her attachment to Ambrosi Pearls, shock tactics had made sense.

She had cared about Ambrosi Pearls like most women cared about their child. From a teenager, she had literally had responsibility shoved at her. She had been so focused on sacrificing herself to make up for the damage her father had done, it was a wonder he had managed to get close to her at all.

He hadn't known every one of those facts when he had walked away from their first engagement, or understood the emotional battering she had taken. He had been so used to seeing her as in charge and ultraorganized that he had overlooked the fact that Sienna, herself, was a victim of her father's gambling problem.

Two years ago he had been coldly angry that Sienna hadn't told him about her father's losses or the loan Roberto had leveraged with his father. He hadn't wanted to address the reason he had reacted so strongly, but he did now.

What he felt for Sienna was different from anything else he had ever experienced.

The thought that she was pregnant, that there would be

a baby, had expanded that feeling out to a second person he could possibly lose.

The constricted emotion in his chest tightened into actual pain. He had always known what that feeling was and the reason why he had been so furious at what he had perceived as Sienna's betrayal.

She was right. He had tried to control her and any children they might have and, in the process, his own emotions. But the legal clauses he had used to bind any children, and thus ensure that Sienna stayed with him, had achieved the exact opposite.

He had ensured that what he needed most, he would lose.

Sixteen

When The Atraeus Group's private jet landed in Sydney it was after eight in the evening and it was raining. After the heat of Medinos, the chill was close to wintry.

Numbly, Sienna refused a ride with Constantine. "I can take a taxi. All I need to do is pick up my car from my mother's house, then I'm driving back to my apartment."

Constantine's expression was grim as he skimmed the airport lounge. "I'll drop you at Pier Point. She'll be expecting it. But if you're not coming home with me—"

"I am not staying with you."

He cupped her elbow and steered her around a baggage cart. "Then stay out at Pier Point." He released her before she could shake free.

Sienna's stomach tightened at the brief, tingling heat of his hold. "If that's an order—"

He massaged the muscles at his nape, the first sign of frustration he'd shown since he had boarded the jet. Up until that moment, he had been frustratingly cool and remote.

"It's not an order, it's a…suggestion." He nodded his head in the direction of the press waiting in the arrival's lounge. Almost immediately the cameras started whirring and the questions started. "And that's why."

Thirty minutes of tense silence later, Constantine parked his Audi in her mother's driveway. He carried her luggage and the briefcase in, then stayed to talk with her mother and Carla for a few minutes. His gaze captured hers while he listened to her mother's stilted congratulations and for a moment she saw past the remote mask he'd maintained to a raw throb of emotion that made her heart pound.

Just before he left, he handed her an envelope. She checked the contents and saw the child custody agreement Vitalis had drawn up torn in two. When she glanced up, Constantine was already gone.

When the sound of the Audi receded, her mother fixed her with a steely glare. "Don't you dare sacrifice yourself for the business, or for us."

Her fingers shaking, she shoved the agreement and the envelope into her purse. "Don't worry, I'm not. If you don't mind, I need a cup of tea." Despite the comfortable flight, the fact that she had faked sleeping meant she had barely eaten or had anything to drink.

Carla frowned and motioned her onto one of the kitchen stools at the counter. "Sit. Talk. I'll make the tea."

Sienna sat and, in between sips of hot tea, concentrated on giving a factual account without the emotional highs and lows. When she'd finished, her mother set a sandwich down in front of her and insisted that she eat.

"To think, I used to like that boy."

Boy? Sienna almost choked on the sandwich. Constantine was six feet four inches of testosterone-laden muscle who could quite possibly have made her pregnant. *Boy* was the last descriptive she would have used.

Margaret Ambrosi lifted an elegant brow. "So did you agree to marry Constantine to save the business?"

"No." She took a bite of the sandwich, forcing it past the tightness in her throat. It was a fact that she wouldn't have agreed to marriage if she didn't love Constantine. "It's complicated."

"You're in love with him. Have been for years."

Sienna's cheeks burned. "Just whose side are you on?"

"Yours. Marry him or don't marry him, but stop worrying about us. If Ambrosi Pearls and this house have to go, so be it, it's your decision. You know Ambrosi Pearls was never my passion."

Sienna stared at the rest of her sandwich, her appetite gone. Constantine had hurt her, deeply enough that she had done nothing but consider refusing to go through with the marriage. After the long, silent flight, and the glimpse of raw loss she had seen in Constantine's gaze, she was almost certain that he would let her go. An ache rose up in her at the thought.

Her mother, with her usual clarity, had cut to the chase. They could survive without Atraeus money. When it came to the crunch, the only question was could she survive without Constantine?

She had told him point-blank on the ride out to Pier Point that she needed time to think things through. He hadn't liked it, but he had accepted her need for space.

That, and the fact that he had surrendered unconditionally on the child custody agreement, constituted progress. She didn't know how long it would take her to heal, but those two things at least signaled a painful step forward.

Her decision settled into place as she slowly sipped her

tea. She could go ahead with the marriage for one simple reason: as hurt as she was she couldn't contemplate not having Constantine in her life.

Two weeks later, the morning of the wedding in Medinos was balmy and relentlessly clear. Although, judging by the pandemonium that had broken out in the last half hour, with cousins, aunts and the hairdresser and makeup team descending en masse, it sounded more like a street riot than a wedding in progress.

Margaret Ambrosi had insisted that if she was getting married in Medinos they needed a house for her to be married from, so Constantine had arranged for a private villa to be made available. It was an old-fashioned idea, but Sienna hadn't minded. The extra fuss and bother had at least taken her mind off the risk she was taking.

Her mother, in combination with Tomas, had pulled all the elements of the wedding together with formidable efficiency, ruthlessly calling in favors to get everything done on time and using Constantine's name to smooth the way. They had organized the dress, the flowers, live music and a church choir, plus a full-scale reception at the *castello*.

Carla poked her head around the door and handed her an envelope. "This arrived for you. Thirty minutes to go. How are you feeling?"

Sienna's heart thumped in her chest as she took the envelope and checked her wristwatch. "Great."

Skittish and unhappy, because she had barely seen him after their stilted conversation the day after arriving in Sydney, when she had agreed to go through with the wedding. When she had, they had never been alone. She was beginning to believe that the loss she had glimpsed in his eyes had been another mirage.

The limousine was booked for eleven; it was ten-thirty.

So far everything had gone without a hitch. Her hair and makeup were done, her jewelry was on and her nails had finally dried.

Her dress was an elegant, sleeveless gown with a scoop neck, simply cut but made of layers of floaty white chiffon that swirled around her ankles as she walked. The petal-soft fabric was a perfect match for the pearl and diamond necklace and earrings her great-aunt had given her as a wedding gift. They were rare, original Ambrosi Pearls pieces.

When Carla shut the door behind her Sienna studied the envelope, her heart thumping hard in her chest when she recognized Constantine's handwriting. When she ripped the envelope open, she found all three copies of the marriage deal she'd signed along with a scribbled note. Constantine hadn't activated the deal or filed any of the paperwork. No shares had changed hands. Ambrosi Pearls was still registered as belonging to her family. The water rights were also enclosed.

In short, he had frozen the entire deal. With the paperwork in her hands she was free to destroy it all if she pleased. To all intents and purposes, it was as if there had never been a deal.

Her legs feeling distinctly wobbly, she sat on the edge of the bed. Constantine had chosen to walk away from exacting any kind of reparations for her father's scam. He now risked financial disaster with his new resort development. She should feel relieved, but all she could think about was, did this mean the wedding was off?

There was a second knock at the door. Carla again, this time with a telephone in one hand. "It's de Vries."

Not Northcliffe as she had expected but Hammond de Vries himself, the CEO of the large European retail conglomerate. The conversation was crisp and to the point.

They had reconsidered, and now wanted to place the order. The sum he offered was staggering. After a short conversation, Sienna hung up and set the phone down just as her mother stepped into the room.

In a lavender suit her mother looked elegant but frazzled. "Sienna—"

The door was pushed wide. Constantine, darkly handsome in a morning suit, stepped past Margaret Ambrosi. "If you'll excuse me, Mrs. Ambrosi, I need to speak to Sienna. Alone."

There was a startled exclamation when Constantine ushered her mother out of the door. "Five minutes," he said smoothly.

Sienna rose to her feet, her heart pounding, because Constantine was dressed for the wedding and because she suddenly knew, beyond doubt, the only fact she needed to know. "I turned de Vries down," she said calmly. "I know you're behind the offer, and I know why you made it."

His gaze was wary. "How did you know it was me?"

"Hammond de Vries doesn't normally call us. One of his buyers does. Besides, they've had my number for months. It was too much of a coincidence that he called today with an offer that would cover the loan. Plus..." She let out a breath. "I happen to know that The Atraeus Group recently bought a percentage of de Vries."

Constantine leaned against the door, his gaze narrowed. "Who told you?"

"An industry contact."

"That would be your mother."

"Who just happened to have a conversation with Tomas—"

His mouth twitched. "—who is putty in her hands."

"Most people are. So...the game's up. You gave me an

out. Or…" She was suddenly afraid to be so ridiculously, luminously happy. "Did you want the out?"

He pushed away from the door, his hands settled at her waist. "By now you have to know what I want. Marriage. But this time it has to be your choice, not just mine."

Sienna wound her arms around Constantine's neck and met his kiss halfway. Long seconds later, he loosened his hold and reached into his pocket. "Just one more thing."

Emotion shimmered through her as he went down on one knee and opened a small, black velvet box. He extracted the ring, a princess-cut white diamond that glowed with an intense, pure fire. "Sienna Ambrosi, will you marry me and be my love?"

Her throat closed on a raw throb, her eyes misted. "Yes."

Constantine slid the ring onto the third finger of her left hand.

"You do love me." Giddy delight spread through her as he rose to his feet and pulled her close. She wound her arms around his neck and held on tight.

He rested his forehead against hers. "I've loved you since the first time I saw you. I can still remember the moment."

"Before the shoe incident?"

"About five seconds before my clumsy attempt at Prince Charming." His mouth curved in a slow smile. "I just had some growing up to do. Make that a lot of growing up."

He bent his head and touched his mouth to hers, and for long seconds she seemed to float. Although the moments of dizziness she had begun to experience in the mornings had an entirely different source.

When he lifted his head and she could breathe again, he ran his hands down her back, molding her against him. The touch was reassuring. She was vulnerable, but so was he; it had just taken him longer to know it.

There was a sharp rap. Margaret Ambrosi's head popped around the side of the door. She wanted to know what was going on, and she wanted to know now.

"It's all right, Mom. The wedding's on."

"Oh, good. I'll inform the limousine driver. I'm sure he'll be delighted, since he's waiting out front."

The door snapped closed, Constantine kissed her again.

Another sharp rap on the door had Sienna pinning on her veil and reaching for her bouquet. She glanced at Constantine, who was showing no signs of moving.

He twined his fingers with hers and gave her another sweet kiss, this time through the veil.

She pushed at his chest. "You need to leave. We'll be late."

"I'm not leaving," he said simply. He tugged her toward the door, a smile in his eyes.

"This time we go together."

* * * * *

PASSION

Harlequin Desire

COMING NEXT MONTH
AVAILABLE MAY 8, 2012

#2155 UNDONE BY HER TENDER TOUCH
Pregnancy & Passion
Maya Banks
When one night with magnate Cam Hollingsworth results in pregnancy, no-strings-attached turns into a tangled web for caterer Pippa Laingley.

#2156 ONE DANCE WITH THE SHEIKH
Dynasties: The Kincaids
Tessa Radley

#2157 THE TIES THAT BIND
Billionaires and Babies
Emilie Rose

#2158 AN INTIMATE BARGAIN
Colorado Cattle Barons
Barbara Dunlop

#2159 RELENTLESS PURSUIT
Lone Star Legacy
Sara Orwig

#2160 READY FOR HER CLOSE-UP
Matchmakers, Inc.
Katherine Garbera

REQUEST YOUR FREE BOOKS!
2 FREE NOVELS PLUS 2 FREE GIFTS!

Harlequin® *Desire*

ALWAYS POWERFUL, PASSIONATE AND PROVOCATIVE

YES! Please send me 2 FREE Harlequin Desire® novels and my 2 FREE gifts (gifts are worth about $10). After receiving them, if I don't wish to receive any more books, I can return the shipping statement marked "cancel." If I don't cancel, I will receive 6 brand-new novels every month and be billed just $4.30 per book in the U.S. or $4.99 per book in Canada. That's a saving of at least 14% off the cover price! It's quite a bargain! Shipping and handling is just 50¢ per book in the U.S. and 75¢ per book in Canada.* I understand that accepting the 2 free books and gifts places me under no obligation to buy anything. I can always return a shipment and cancel at any time. Even if I never buy another book, the two free books and gifts are mine to keep forever.

225/326 HDN FEF3

Name _____ (PLEASE PRINT)

Address _____ Apt. #

City _____ State/Prov. _____ Zip/Postal Code

Signature (if under 18, a parent or guardian must sign)

Mail to the **Reader Service:**
IN U.S.A.: P.O. Box 1867, Buffalo, NY 14240-1867
IN CANADA: P.O. Box 609, Fort Erie, Ontario L2A 5X3

Not valid for current subscribers to Harlequin Desire books.

Want to try two free books from another line?
Call 1-800-873-8635 or visit www.ReaderService.com.

* Terms and prices subject to change without notice. Prices do not include applicable taxes. Sales tax applicable in N.Y. Canadian residents will be charged applicable taxes. Offer not valid in Quebec. This offer is limited to one order per household. All orders subject to credit approval. Credit or debit balances in a customer's account(s) may be offset by any other outstanding balance owed by or to the customer. Please allow 4 to 6 weeks for delivery. Offer available while quantities last.

Your Privacy—The Reader Service is committed to protecting your privacy. Our Privacy Policy is available online at www.ReaderService.com or upon request from the Reader Service.

We make a portion of our mailing list available to reputable third parties that offer products we believe may interest you. If you prefer that we not exchange your name with third parties, or if you wish to clarify or modify your communication preferences, please visit us at www.ReaderService.com/consumerschoice or write to us at Reader Service Preference Service, P.O. Box 9062, Buffalo, NY 14269. Include your complete name and address.

HDES11B

New York Times *and* USA TODAY *bestselling author*
Maya Banks presents book four in her miniseries
PREGNANCY & PASSION

UNDONE BY HER TENDER TOUCH

Available May 2012 from Harlequin® Desire!

"**W**ould you like some help?"

Pippa whirled around, still holding the bottle of champagne, and darn near tossed the contents onto the floor.

"Help?"

Cam nodded slowly. "Assistance? You look as though you could use it. How on earth did you think you'd manage to cater this event on your own?"

Pippa was horrified by his offer and then, as she processed the rest of his statement, she was irritated as hell.

"I'd hate for you to sully those pretty hands," she snapped. "And for your information, I've got this under control. The help didn't show. Not my fault. The food is impeccable, if I do say so myself. I just need to deliver it to the guests."

"I believe I just offered my assistance and you insulted me," Cam said dryly.

Her eyebrows drew together. Oh, why did the man have to be so damn delicious-looking? And why could she never perform the simplest functions around him?

"You're Ashley's guest," Pippa said firmly. "Not to mention you're used to being served, not serving others."

"How do you know what I'm used to?" he asked mildly.

She had absolutely nothing to say to that and watched in bewilderment as he hefted the tray up and walked out of the kitchen.

She sagged against the sink, her pulse racing hard enough

to make her dizzy.

Cameron Hollingsworth was gorgeous, unpolished in a rough and totally sexy way, arrogant and so wrong for her. But there was something about the man that just did it for her.

She sighed. He was a luscious specimen of a male and he couldn't be any less interested in her.

Even so, she was itching to shake his world up a little.

Realizing she was spending far too much time mooning over Cameron, she grabbed another tray, took a deep breath to compose herself and then headed toward the living room.

And Cameron Hollingsworth.

Will Pippa shake up Cameron's world?
Find out in Maya Banks's passionate new novel

UNDONE BY HER TENDER TOUCH

Available May 2012 from Harlequin® Desire!